Book I

HAIL MURPHY!

We who are about to die,
salute you!

Arthur Whiteson, the president of the United States of America, stared at the three people assembled around him at the oval conference table. All three of them shifted under his fierce gaze.

Whiteson breathed deeply, monitoring himself. What had he said a few moments ago to these idiotic geniuses? Oh, yes, that they should be hung by chains for eternity so they could think about what they had done. Had these people *ever* thought of safeguards?

The Star Bright project was relentlessly following Murphy's Laws. The fusion experiment was indeed going from bad to worse and moving inexorably to uncontrollable.

A week earlier Dr. Richard Clayton and Dr. Lawrence Pound had realized that the fusion fire that they had ignited and contained in a sheath of pure magnetic force was growing.

Well, that hadn't been so bad, not by itself. But then they discovered they couldn't put out the fire. And a white-faced Kathy Farrel, turning slowly from omnipotent computers, had dropped another bomb in their midst.

Not only could the fire not be put out, but *there seemed to be no limit as to how much it would keep growing.*

Murphy's Laws reigned supreme.

Novels by MARTIN CAIDIN

Beamriders
Prison Ship
The God Machine
Four Came Back
Manfac
Three Corners to
  Nowhere
Exit Earth
Zoboa
The Messiah Stone
Killer Station
Marooned
No Man's World
The Cape
Starbright
Jericho 52
Aquarius Mission

Cyborg
Operation Nuke
High Crystal
Devil Take All
The Last Dogfight
Anytime, Anywhere
Whip
The Last Fathom
The Mendelov
  Conspiracy
Almost Midnight
Maryjane Tonight at
  Angels 12
Wingborn
The Final Countdown
Deathmate
The Long Night
Cyborg IV

MARTIN CAIDIN

STAR BRIGHT

BAEN BOOKS

A Baen Book

Baen Publishing Enterprises
260 Fifth Avenue
New York, N.Y. 10001

ISBN: 0-671-69858-3

Cover art by Ken Kelly

First printing, January 1990

Distributed by
SIMON & SCHUSTER
1230 Avenue of the Americas
New York, N.Y. 10020

Printed in the United States of America

1

The sweep hand came around to the top of the watch. In the darkness, Jace Wilson studied the luminous dial and nodded to himself. Three o'clock precisely—time to start moving. He stared into the night, trying to see the three other agents in the mottled gloom. He knew that they had also looked up from their watches and tried to catch sight of one another. No way in these eye-twisting moon shadows, he thought. So much the better. They'd be impossible to spot by anyone else.

From their separate positions, the four men started up the slope. They cursed inwardly as they struggled up the incline. It was a bitch. The grass was damp, making climbing slippery and treacherous. The house toward which they moved stood atop the hill, a hulking outline, its windows reflecting the thin moonlight. One man snapped a branch, and the sound cracked in the night air. As if a switch had been thrown, a dog in the house barked. Damn. They knew about the animal. It was a German shepherd, a trained guard dog. The four men tensed. If the animal got loose, it would come down the slope after them. They didn't want to hurt the dog; they didn't want to hurt anything or anyone. Their only purpose was to make certain no one left that house by the back or the side entrances. That was all. None of them were armed with weapons.

The dog continued to bark, and the agents stayed where they were, waiting. Then they had their break. A jet boomed away from the St. Cloud airport, drenching the night with its own sound. They didn't waste the opportunity. They scrambled up the rest of the slope, using bushes, branches, the ground itself for leverage. Breathing heavily, they rested where they had stopped near the rear of the house. Jace Wilson pressed a skin tape against his lips. A neat gimmick, that, he thought—flat wiring, circuitry printed right into the flesh-colored tape. The wiring ran invisibly to another piece of skin tape within his left ear.

"Three here. Report." Voices trickled into his ear. The other men were in position. He waited. Other people had been listening to the exchange, and one of them finally called in. "One here. We're moving."

That would be Tom Harlan; another agent would be with him. In the darkness, his back against a tree for comfortable leverage, Jace Wilson envisioned Harlan and the other man walking toward the front door of the house. The address was 28 Waverly Drive, St. Cloud, Colorado. It was a tall stone structure that had been there for years. Professor Owen Kimberly lived there alone, except for the dog and a housekeeper who showed up at eight every morning. Jace Wilson studied his watch again. Right on schedule. He knew there were agents in cars and trucks to the east and west of the house, along Waverly Drive. He hoped none of them would be necessary.

Footsteps sounded along the flagstone walk. Jace Wilson waited, timing it all in his head. A doorbell sounded, and instantly the dog barked furiously.

The agents heard a voice commanding the animal. There was immediate silence, then the sound of the front door opening. Tom Harlan said his apologies smoothly. He was wired for sound, and Jace Wilson, in the darkness by the back door to the house, heard every word.

"My identification, sir." Tom Harlan loomed in the doorway of Professor Owen Kimberly's home and presented his ID wallet. It was all there in the light from the foyer. Name, photograph, the federal seal, the name of the group he represented— the National Security Agency. Owen Kimberly was a bigger man than Harlan had expected.

Kimberly casually pushed his tousled salt-and-pepper hair away from his glasses. He shuffled to one side and waved the two men into his home. "Come in, come in, man," he chided the security agent. "It's much too cold to be standing out there like that." He closed the door behind them, smiling tolerantly as the two men gazed suspiciously at the huge dog.

"Stay." At the one-word command, the animal sank at once to the floor, resting his great head on his forepaws. But his eyes followed every move.

"He won't bother you," Kimberly offered as he led the way to a library off the main room. "It's

late," he went on as he turned on the library
lights, "and I'm sure you're as tired as I am. Do
you want coffee? I'm not much of a host, but I
could make some instant."

Tom Harlan shook his head. "No, thank you,
sir." He stood comfortably, watching Kimberly set-
tle his bulk into an easy chair.

"Do sit down, please," Kimberly urged. "You
make me uncomfortable with all that standing. It
reminds me of days long ago when I wore a uniform and marched in parades." He gestured to the
second man. "You do have a name of your own, I
presume?"

"Yes, sir. Jack Smith."

"How clever," Kimberly mused. He turned back
to Harlan who now sat straight-backed on the edge
of the couch. Kimberly smiled to himself. Why
did security people give themselves away so much
through such actions? A long time ago Owen
Kimberly had dealt with enough people in security to recognize the signs. It was painfully obvious
that this Harlan fellow was on his best behavior,
trying in every small way to please. If Harlan had
been anything less than under some tremendous
strain, he would at least have leaned back comfortably in his seat. But he remained as taut as a
bowstring.

"I presume you'd like to get right to the matter
of this, ah, unusual call?" Kimberly made a steeple
of his fingers and observed Tom Harlan as if study-
ing the man along a rifle sight.

Harlan looked back and seemed to recognize for
the first time just how completely self-possessed
this man was. "Yes, sir. The head of the agency
requested I make this call personally."

"I had already assumed that by your presence."

Harlan absorbed the needle easily. "Yes, sir. I've been ordered to ask—to *ask*, sir—that you accompany me to Washington without delay. It is a matter of the greatest urgency, Professor Kimberly. National security at the highest level is involved, and—"

"Is that why you surrounded my home, Mr. Harlan?" Kimberly made no attempt to hide the touch of sandpaper in his tone. "To *ask* me?"

"I apologize, sir."

"You do so too smoothly. There seems an inherent lack of sincerity in your remark."

Tom Harlan frowned. He hadn't expected this, hadn't expected anything like this at all. The ball had somehow been snatched from his hands before he had done more than broach the purpose of his nocturnal call. Harlan showed interest. "Would you—ah—mind telling us how you knew?"

Kimberly waved his hand in a diffident gesture. "Child's play, Mr. Harlan, and I mean the word literally and without so much as a stab at modesty. Infrared sweep patterns, laser interrupters, ultrasensitive microphones underground and in the trees. More of a hobby than anything else. There's little in this place worth a major break-in. Why don't you tell your people to leave that back slope? It's damp and chilly out there tonight, and they'll catch their death of cold." Kimberly's smile grew. "But you don't need to tell them anything, do you? You're wired for sound, of course." The last statement came without a touch of question to his words.

Tom Harlan sighed. His back yielded perhaps an inch as he settled more heavily onto the couch.

"All right, Jace, tell your people to pick up their marbles and wait in their vehicles."

Kimberly laughed aloud, then frowned. Someone was going to an enormous amount of trouble to find him—reaching into his home, setting up a complicated system to throw a net about him, while also handling him with kid gloves. Well, get on with it then, he thought.

"This is most entertaining, Mr. Harlan, but please get to the reason for your visit."

Harlan shifted again in his seat, snapping back to his former rigid position. "Yes, sir. As I was saying, I've been directed to request your presence in Washington. The National Security Council. From Adrian Russel personally."

"I know him."

Harlan kept his features unchanged. "Yes, sir. Mr. Russel gave me a letter I am to hand you." He reached into his jacket pocket, withdrew a sealed envelope, and handed it to Kimberly. Kimberly accepted the envelope, then dropped it unopened on the end table by his chair. He offered no explanation for leaving it unread.

"Do go on," he urged the perplexed NSA agent.

"Well, it's—I mean, the pressure is really on, professor. It took us several days to find you. I—"

"Do you mean to tell me that giving up my security clearance made it *that* difficult? I *am* disappointed in you, Mr. Harlan." Kimberly chuckled. "You needed only to study any academic registry to know where I was. But I imagine," he said more slowly, "you had to follow your cloak-and-dagger routine. It's unimportant, really. Tell me what *is* important."

"Sir?"

"Why is Adrian Russel so eager to see me?"

"It's in his letter, I imagine."

"You imagine. You don't know for sure?"

"No, sir."

"Interesting. But you do know the general reason, I daresay."

A muscle moved in Harlan's cheek. "Yes, sir."

"Tell me, then."

"Aren't you going to open the letter, professor?"

"No."

"Might I ask why not, sir?"

"If Adrian Russel wishes to talk with me, it is much wiser for him, and certainly more courteous, to either pick up his telephone and call me or to visit me personally. Since he has done neither, Mr. Harlan, I must reject the imperative nature you give his letter."

"But I—"

"You were saying you knew the general subject, Mr. Harlan."

The NSA man shook his head, bewildered. Owen Kimberly had summarily dismissed the most powerful security man—and a scientist in his own right—with scarcely a wave of his hand. Tom Harlan was an outstanding security agent, but he was finding himself boxed in by this strange man, and he was finding it increasingly difficult to extricate himself. It was all going badly. Harlan knew his approach lacked the deftness and the psychological overtures this situation required, but he had no time to spare.

What he knew of the situation was sufficiently terrifying for him to lack understanding of this man's diffidence. Harlan did not frighten easily, and for several days he had lived with a fear alien to him. Now he was confused. If this man had only an inkling of what was happening! But Harlan was a security agent, a director, in fact, and he could do nothing other than to ignore the dictates of common sense and stand by the rules that commanded his silence. He couldn't break his own ties, his regulations. He couldn't—even in the face of the most appalling threat the world had known—violate that by which he lived.

Dr. Owen Kimberly was not a man who could be prodded with hints of dark secrets. As a younger scientist, such hinted overtures might have immediately compelled his interest and made him willing to accompany the NSA agent. But that was long ago. Now, Harlan faced a tall and relaxed man to whom the term *individual* meant everything. Cherishing his sense of himself, dedicated to his teaching, and utterly devoted to his fiancée Angela and her children, he had erected a great wall against men like Tom Harlan and the governmental monolith they represented.

"I can't break security, Professor Kimberly. I'm sorry, truly, but I must go by my orders." Tom Harlan knew he was handling the situation badly, but he saw no way out of the moment.

"Then, Mr. Harlan, I will respond in kind. *I* must go by the dictates of my conscience and by my feelings of distaste for a government that has not yet discovered how to be forthright and honest. I would suggest you pass on my very fond personal regards to Adrian Russel, and, if you wish, you may return his letter. Unopened, of course."

Harlan forced himself to release his fingernails from where they had dug into the palms of his hands. He took several long, deep breaths. He just couldn't return to Washington with that message!

"I don't think you understand how serious all this is, professor." Harlan knew a touch of steel was edging in to his voice, but he couldn't help it. This man couldn't be that much of a fool. "Look, professor, this whole thing is terrifying. It's got the top people in Washington and in Tennessee ready to climb walls and—"

The expression on Kimberly's face brought him up short. There was no pleasure there. "So that's it," Owen Kimberly said softly. "You're in trouble on the fusion project."

His words seemed to sting Harlan. The NSA man jerked visibly. "I didn't say that," he said hastily.

"For God's sake, throw away your cloak and dagger," came the retort. "This isn't a guessing game for brownie points, Mr. Harlan. It's obvious there's trouble somewhere. I know my own research background. You know it as well, I'm sure," he added drily, "and you're here in the middle of the night, acting as if your jockstrap is binding you. You needed only to mention Washington and Tennessee to put everything out on the table."

Kimberly pushed aside the problems of Tom Harlan and thought of what was going on in the Cumberland research reservation. Trouble, very obviously. How much, what kind? All that was conjecture, and he doubted that he'd learn much from this paragon of security before him.

"I'm sure it's all quite interesting," Kimberly said, and he rose to his feet. The other men stood

at once, slightly uncomfortable with Kimberly staring down at them. "But you already have my
answer, don't you?"

Harlan stared at him with open disbelief. "I
can't believe you're so callous about all this," he
snapped.

"Callous? You do me an injustice, Mr. Harlan. I
left government research many years ago. I haven't
had a thing to—"

"You don't understand, Kimberly! We *need* you!
Project Star Bright's gone mad. It's—"

Kimberly's interruption was almost gentle. "Forgive me," he said. "I know what it's called, Mr.
Harlan. After all, a long time ago I gave that
project its name."

Hope flared in Harlan's eyes. "Then you *know*
why you must come with me."

For the first time, Owen Kimberly's patience
thinned. "I don't know anything of the sort," he
said with a touch of anger. "And I'm tired of your
word games. More to the point, Harlan, I really
don't give a tinker's damn about the fusion project
or its problems. I told you I left government research many years ago. Perhaps I should have
added, although there's no question you already
know it, that I left all contact with my government
behind me. Except, of course, to pay taxes. Now
I've had enough of all this. The sooner you leave
here the shorter your return trip to Washington
will be. I—"

Kimberly paused, his thoughts racing furiously.
Project Star Bright was hardly a secret. The
newspapers and television had saturated the country with reports of igniting the first thermonuclear

flame in a laboratory. Fusion fire under control. The wonders of tomorrow here today. No more energy shortage. Over and over again he had read and heard the stories about the Cumberland research center in Tennessee where they were duplicating the fire that burned within the sun.

And something was wrong, perhaps drastically. But, Kimberly thought, he couldn't tell how wrong from this security android in his home, no matter how intense his agitation. And Kimberly had an almost savage dislike of generalities, hints, and shadows. Yet, he admitted to himself, he had secretly waited a long time for this very moment. For years he had hoped that the Cumberland scientists would come a cropper in their damned fusion program so they would have to read again what he had written years ago, and they would have to turn to him for whatever salvation lay beyond their own grasp. Here, at last, was the moment that could give him the sweet joy of reading the riot act to a member of the same system that had once nearly destroyed him. And, he smiled to himself, he had almost committed the folly of doing just that.

It's no longer necessary, he thought. A man finds peace and respect and love, and who needs the shouting and the rest of it? In three days Angela and I will be married, and her children will have a father who loves them, who needs their love just as much as they need his. He remembered an old saying. *A professional never gets angry. He just gets even.* But the best way to get even is to live well. And I live very well, indeed. Life is more than generous to me. I am blessed with Angela. I can't, I won't, leave her or this place.

Kimberly walked to the library door and turned. "Please," he said to Tom Harlan and the other man with him. "Just go away."

2

Arthur Whiteson, the president of the United States of America, sat rigidly in his upholstered chair, aware suddenly that the back of his shirt was wet with perspiration and that he could feel the leather of the chair through his shirt. He leaned back in his chair, forcing himself to relax. He stared at the three people assembled around him at the oval conference table, then looked up at the morning sun shining through the window drapes. He listened to the chopping sounds of nearby helicopter blades. He did not want to face the unthinkable.

Arthur Whiteson shook his head and said, "Oh, shit." The three people at the table looked startled.

He drummed his fingers on the thick oak table. Strange, those maniacs seated with him appeared more upset over the president swearing than they were with the problem they faced. Problem? My God, what an inadequate, useless, senseless, stupid word.

President Whiteson leaned forward. With his

shirtsleeves rolled up, he felt the cool wood on his forearms. Momentarily he glanced down and started, as if for the first time, at the thick hair curling over the muscles of his arm. He flexed his arm and saw muscle emerge in relief. He looked up.

"You are perhaps the most dangerous people I have ever known, or known of, in my entire life. If I could, if I could do it, I would have you all shackled to a wall somewhere and left there for all eternity. But even then I doubt there would be enough time for you to understand just what the hell you have done."

All three of them shifted under his fierce gaze. Whiteson looked from one to the other. At the opposite end of the table squirmed Dr. Lawrence Pound of the Atomic Energy Commission, the director of Project Star Bright. To Whiteson's left sat Dr. Richard Clayton, chief scientist of Star Bright, and to his right sat Dr. Kathy Farrel, a brilliant programmer and alter ego to Dr. Clayton. President Whiteson realized he must come to know, in the next several minutes, just what these people thought, what they felt, and what they really *knew*, if there was to be even a slight hope of salvation from what they had created.

Dr. Pound was predictable enough—a typical government scientist in his sixties, cut from much the same mold as thousands of other government scientists and project managers. They could easily have been stamped out from the same press and then had small and variable personality traits added. There he sat in all his miserable little glory, addicted, in the old English-German tradition, to tweed jackets and pipe-smoking badges of office and seniority. Yet once, a long time ago, he had been a reliable scientist and since then about as capable an administrator as anyone really had the right to expect. He stood perhaps five feet ten inches in height and with his paunch would have made a perfect example for male corset ads.

However, President Whiteson did not want to be unfair about Larry Pound. He had been a technical assistant in the Chicago laboratory beneath the squash court when the first nuclear reactions in the experimental pile had begun to click faster and faster, and they had all heard the distant rumbling of the atomic genie about to break free of its bottle. Three years later precisely that had happened. By July of 1945, Lawrence Pound had become a young scientist in his own right, and he was part of the team that assembled the first atomic bomb and watched it sunder the Alamogordo dawn with a cleaver of a hundred million degrees and a blow of light that screamed with its terrible glare.

Bikini Atoll, Eniwetok Atoll, Jackass Flats. One by one the names rolled into history with tests of more powerful bombs, then hydrogen bombs and superbombs, and Dr. Lawrence Pound slowly and steadily —gaining seniority simply by being there— climbed the administrative ladder. When controlled thermonuclear fusion—trying to duplicate under laboratory conditions the process by which the sun burns its own fuel—became a major government project, the head of the AEC tapped Pound for the job as director. It was a good choice, reflected President Whiteson, for the director had to be careful, knowledgeable, and reliable. This man with the pipe and the tweed suit was—if nothing else— just that.

Which wasn't enough, not by a million light years, to handle what had happened with Star Bright. Dr. Lawrence Pound was the shepherd who found atop the mountain not his flock of sheep, but a monstrous fire-breathing dragon with a voracious appetite.

Whiteson dismissed Pound; he would not be an important element in finding a solution to what Star Bright had wrought. But he *would* be useful for all his years of contacts and associations, of being able to slice through bureaucratic red tape. And, *that*, noted the president, was going to become more necessary than it had *ever* been.

The second man was of special interest to the president. Dr. Richard Clayton was a product of the new age, the amalgam of different disciplines producing a new strain of scientist terribly expert and capable in a single field, with some peripheral attachments, but all too often woefully shut off from anything else that made up the real world. Although brilliant, he was an innocent child wandering through the fast-moving traffic lanes of everyday life.

There existed, however, a worthwhile relationship between Pound and Dr. Clayton. The younger man was the administrator's prize scientist, a man recognized early in his career as a true genius. Clayton was moved carefully through the lower ranks of research efforts, and from then on he moved with speed and brilliance. Under the parental protection of Pound, he became the one man more than any other responsible for making of Star Bright a blazing fire instead of a paper-chain theory.

Clayton, the president noted with more than

idle interest, was surprisingly young for his position as chief scientist of Star Bright. And, brooded Arthur Whiteson, it was that very mixture of young age and genius that was part of the problem. Genius was simply no substitute for experience. Being blessed with the smarts, the president thought to himself, was a long way from *being* smart. Clayton's extensive knowledge in the areas of electromagnetic force fields, nuclear physics, astrophysics, and thermonuclear reactions research was dazzling. But this knowledge also made him a supremely dangerous man, dabbling as he did with supremely powerful forces.

More than any other man, Dr. Richard Clayton was responsible for the basic design of the magnetic "bottle" apparatus that contained the terrible fire of nuclear fusion. However, if pressed by someone with knowledge and experience in the field, he would admit, with some unscientific toe scuffing, that he had gained his solid grounding in that field from reading the obscure and nearly forgotten research papers of Professor Owen Kimberly, long departed from the scene of active thermonuclear research.

President Whiteson tried to put together the many pieces of Richard Clayton into a single entity he could predict and manage. Sitting almost ramrod straight in his chair, Richard Clayton was a man with such a sharply defined face it seemed almost to be a true cameo in appearance. He was just shy of six feet in height, strangely thin in the chest, yet with great bony shoulders. President Whiteson knew the essential details of Clayton's personal life as well. The man who was a pure mental calculator in the laboratory was often bland in his bed and in his home. Clayton had a wife, two children, and a dog in the back yard—the proper statistical mixture—and the president would have bet even money that if pressed, Dick Clayton would not have been able to provide a detailed, clear description of what his wife looked like.

Whiteson turned his thoughts to the third person in the room, Dr. Kathy Farrel, the woman who spent more time with Clayton than Mrs. Clayton did. Yet appearances were deceiving, for Kathy was utterly, totally devoted to, not the man, but the scientist, and she basked in the glory of being alter ego to Richard Clayton. Many years before, she had begun working as his scientific aide, secretary, and Girl Friday, as well as specializing in her own career as a computer programmer. Through the years she had expanded both careers until, working with the great cybernetics systems they used to augment human brainpower, she became as brilliant in programming as Clayton was in basic and applied research. It was actually a splendid association, enhancing the capabilities of each, and creating a sort of two-brain gestalt in which their joined brain-power was far greater than simply the sum of two individual parts. In spite of his genius, Dr. Clayton still remained almost wholly dependent in his work upon the performance of the great electronic brains of computers. Kathy Farrel understood the mind of Clayton as well as the machinations of her "pet brains" made of steel, glass, magnetic force fields, and God knew what else. Thus she functioned as Clayton's bridge between his own genius and the superfast computer systems.

Not that she looked like it, thought President

Whiteson. She was in her early thirties, strikingly attractive, her clothes not at all concealing her full bust and shapely lines. If she and Clayton had ever been to bed, judged President Whiteson, it had been a matter of convenience rather than desire. Any affair that ever started between those two was condemned to be one way only. Dr. Clayton was totally absorbed, mesmerized as it were, by the imminence of his success and impending fame as a result of his years-long efforts to light the thermonuclear furnace.

There was a danger with those two individuals that President Whiteson had tried to identify from the outset of first meeting them. They were so capable, so powerful in the scientific sense, that they were vulnerable to some of the more essential groundings in this business. Coming to trust a computer totally left them exposed to faulty reasoning, for the computer was essentially a mindless creature that did not reason.

Whiteson chuckled to himself—and was instantly amazed that any part of his own mind could still squeeze amusement from gross horror—as he recalled a story regarding one of the more emphatic absurdities of pure scientific deduction. There was once a scientist working at the space center in Florida who, tired of his brain-squeezing efforts, amused himself with a hobby that required him to train a flea to jump on verbal command. Dedicated, studious, patient, he succeeded admirably in training the tiny pet to leap at his bidding. But as heavy minds are so often inclined to do, he tired of sport and chose the predictable path of changing hobby to experiment.

He removed the front two legs from the flea and

commanded his miniscule charge to jump. Well-trained and as obedient as any dog, the flea jumped. Then he removed the center two legs and again gave the command to jump. Once more the flea leaped from its surface. Finally the scientist removed the last two legs from his faithful charge and cried, "Jump!"

The flea, of course, did no such thing, which prompted the learned scientist to write a report to the effect that when you remove all six legs from a flea, it loses its sense of hearing.

President Whiteson breathed deeply, monitoring himself. What had he said a few moments ago to these idiotic geniuses? Oh, yes, that they should be hung by chains for eternity so they could think about what they had done. Had these people *ever* thought of safeguards? Had they ever considered they might be wrong in what they were doing and that the consequences of not being right could be utterly catastrophic?

The Star Bright project was relentlessly following Murphy's Laws. The first law states that what can go wrong *will* go wrong. That had already happened. The second law holds that what is already wrong is bound to get worse. The fusion project was indeed going from bad to worse and moving inexorably to uncontrollable.

Arthur Whiteson had to determine how long that would take, what the consequences were if they failed, and how much time it required to stave off the inevitable. Again he chided himself. How do you stave off the inevitable? he demanded of his own thoughts. With work, brains, and an enormous faith in whatever deity shaped human affairs on this stray little planet.

A week earlier Dr. Richard Clayton and Dr. Lawrence Pound had realized that the fusion fire that they had ignited and contained in a sheath of pure magnetic force was growing.

Well, that hadn't been so bad, not by itself. But then they discovered they couldn't put out the fire. And a white-faced Kathy Farrel, turning slowly from omnipotent computers, had dropped another bomb in their midst.

Not only could the fire not be put out, but *there seemed to be no limit as to how much it would keep growing*.

Murphy's Laws reigned supreme.

"I want to tell you people something," President Arthur Whiteson said suddenly, catching the three people with him unawares so that they all jumped slightly. "The United States faces today, as it seems to face every year, a great number of problems. We are under pressure from the world community and pressure from within. That's our lot in life, it's a way of life. It's *my* way of life."

He pursed his lips for a moment. "In my own front yard, there are people trying to hang me for this new round of inflation," he continued. "In addition, we've got a new tinderbox ignited in Asia, and we're so deep in three wars in Africa they're reaching over our ears. The black revolution has become a brown revolution to such an extent that it's the whites against *everybody* else. Those are all problems we're supposed to handle."

There seemed to be no way to prevent the bitterness from seeping into his voice. He hated hearing the acidity in his tone, but Jesus Christ, there was that political faction bolting the party, the Russians had come up with a new brace of weapons that had the Pentagon pounding on his doors, the isolationists were in full cry because the United States was embroiled in four wars, and—

"And," he said aloud, "all you people are trying to do is to set the goddamned planet on fire."

Making no attempt to keep the steel from his words, he said, "Now you will tell me what will happen if you fail to put out that fire." He hesitated only a moment. "And *don't* start looking to one another for your answers!" he snapped. "Dammit, look at me and answer my questions! You first, Dr. Clayton."

Every feature of the cameo face had frozen. "There are a number of possibilities," Clayton said finally.

"Name them," Arthur Whiteson ordered.

"It could go out by itself, and—"

"You don't know that, do you?"

"No, sir."

"Then, man, tell me what you *do* know!"

Clayton shifted uncomfortably. "I wish I could, Mr. President. But there's nothing we really know for certain. I—"

"Except that it's burning down there in Cumberland."

"Yes, sir."

"What are the odds it will extinguish itself, for lack of fuel, or—or—or *what?*"

"We don't know for sure," Clayton said miserably.

"I don't believe, Mr. President," Kathy Farrel broke in, "there's much hope for that."

"Is that a computer readout, Dr. Farrel?"

She didn't yield before him. "No, sir."

"Then?"

"The fact that it has burned this long means it may be feeding on anything."

"Be more specific."

"It could be feeding on terrestrial mass, from atmospheric nuclei, or from the magnetic bottle itself." She pressed her lips firmly together before speaking again. "It could be creating a force field and feeding upon itself."

He stared at her. "What you say sounds quite mad."

"Yes, sir, but it's a possibility as real as any other."

"I appreciate your candor. Can your computers come up with anything to help?"

She shook her head. "Not yet, Mr. President. There are too many unknowns. My staff is feeding every scrap of information, even as we're determining new characteristics of the fire, into the computer systems. We're on a constant readout of new data, and the out-tapes are monitored at all times. The first indication of anything, of anything at all, would help."

The woman had more balls than the two men put together, he judged.

"Dr. Pound, you've been in the business a long time, you know other people who've done research in fusion research. Can you think of anyone you should bring into this? You would have absolute priority."

Dr. Lawrence Pound wanted desperately for his heart to cease its mad pounding. He was certain they had all heard it, that they held him in contempt for the noise he knew his heart was making in this closed room. He was closer to panic than anyone realized. It had always been his dream to sit in this room with the man who was the president of the nation, and now that he was here, his heart thundered in his frail chest, and he fought to keep his bladder from betraying him. He shook his head slowly, staring down at the table.

"N-no, sir. But, I am thinking about it, Mr. President."

Arthur Whiteson's voice crashed through Pound's self-pity. "Isn't there *anyone* who knows what to do about this thing?" he demanded. He ignored Pound; the old bastard would hardly be able to walk out of the room as it was. "Miss Farrel, I know something about the business. A fire, any kind of fire, simply does not continue burning at a static rate. It's either going to die out, as I hope fervently, or—"

He paused, and she stepped in. "Yes, sir. If it doesn't diminish, it—it must grow."

"If growth is the next step," Whiteson said with icy calm, "does it have a limit?"

"I will not lie, Mr. President. It is unpredictable."

"Marvelous," he said, his voice a deep whisper that nevertheless carried across the room.

He didn't miss the sudden, brief look Kathy Farrel gave Clayton. It was a look that betrayed great thought and conflict. He watched her turn her gaze back to him.

"Mr. President, there is one man who—" Her voice cut off in mid-sentence. Just her tone bespoke stirrings far deeper than indicated by her words, and that tone had galvanized Clayton into a sudden anger. He kept his silence, glaring at her.

For the moment, Whiteson ignored the electrical exchange. "Who are you referring to, Dr. Farrel?"

"I—I had started to say there was one man who might—"

"He's been out of research for years!" Clayton snapped.

Arthur Whiteson had had more than enough. "Dr. Clayton, shut up. I'm ordering you to keep your mouth closed."

Clayton stared at him in shocked disbelief. Whiteson kept his eyes locked on Kathy Farrel. "Continue what you were saying."

"There was one man who did a great deal of theoretical research in fusion power," she said carefully. "I have always felt he—well—he was more responsible than any other person for getting Star Bright into the project stage."

"His name," Whiteson urged.

"Dr. Owen Kimberly."

Seeing the fury on Clayton's face, Whiteson was taken aback. "I presume you don't like Kimberly, Dr. Clayton?"

"Yes, sir."

"Is he as good as Dr. Farrel indicates? No personalities, doctor."

"That's a matter of opinion, Mr. President."

"To hell with your opinion, then. Give me your professional judgment, and you will answer to me personally if I find personal prejudice involved here."

Dr. Clayton took a long breath, then let it out in a shuddering exhalation. "He—he did more research than anyone else. He went into areas we've never explored."

The president remained silent, thinking carefully. Dr. Owen Kimberly. That was the man that Adrian Russel over at NSA had spoken of. Russel had said that Kimberly was as much at home in the complex world of thermonuclear energy as a mechanic was with a car. They had talked about bringing Kimberly to Washington to—

Whiteson pressed a button on the side of the table, and almost as quickly as his hand left the button a secretary came through a door to his side. "Adrian Russel at NSA. Get him on the line for me. Break into anything he's doing."

"Yes, sir." The door closed. They sat in silence, waiting. A light flashed on the telephone, and immediately Whiteson picked it up.

"Adrian? Good. Let me get right down to business. Do you remember the man we discussed the other day? Owen Kimberly? Yes, that's right. What's happened with that? I believe you said you were sending some people to bring him to Washington. What? Yes. By all means, let me hear what happened."

Whiteson's face took on a darker hue as he listened to the other man on the telephone. Finally the president spoke again. "Just stand by, Adrian."

His eyes showed stark disbelief as he looked at the three people with him. Covering the mouthpiece with one hand, he said, "They sent some people to bring Kimberly here."

"I'm sure he can help," Kathy Farrel said, her smile brightening.

"He refused to come," the president added.

They were startled. "How? That—that's impossible," Clayton burst out. "Once he knew what happened, he couldn't—"

"They didn't tell him," Whiteson said slowly.

"It would have been a violation of security. So he sent them away."

Kathy Farrel's hand flew to her mouth, but not soon enough to stifle completely the laugh that burst from her. The president studied her for a long moment. "Thank you, Dr. Farrel, for being so honest. If I could, I'd join in your laughter." He brought the phone back to his mouth.

"Adrian, listen carefully. The instant you hang up your telephone your only duty in this world is to bring Owen Kimberly to me. To me directly, do you understand? He's to talk with no one else, he's to be brought here no matter what time of day or night, no matter what I'm doing, no matter with whom I may be. Did you get all that? Get him. I don't care how or what you have to do or who you have to hurt, just don't hurt *him*.

"What's that, Adrian? Listen to me. If Owen Kimberly isn't here in twenty-four hours, don't bother going back to your office. *Ever*. Because you're fired at the end of those twenty-four hours."

3

Deep in the rolling, tree-forested hills of Cumberland, Tennessee, within the confines of a heavily secured government reservation, the fire burned.

It was a fire—for it could not be called a flame—like no other in the history of the planet. It burned as do the fires that rage in the hearts of suns, small or large. It was a burning of total energy, a transformation of matter in a process no man could see with the naked eye.

Enclosed in a magnetic sheath, it was not free in the thick ocean of atmospheric gases. Had such freedom been permitted, the shock wave would have been terrifying, because the fire no man could look at, or really describe, burned with a temperature of a hundred million degrees. That is a temperature beyond all human meaning. It is a fire for which we possess no description. It is the kind of fire that makes the flames with which we are familiar—in steel mills, in fireplaces, in acetylene torches—icy cold in comparison.

It is the fire with which God shaped His universe, the fire of Creation.

It was impossible. There was no reason known to man or science for this fire to exist. It could not do so. It violated every law of physics and matter and energy. A sun, after all, is a ball, a sphere of immense size and overwhelming mass, a clash of inward gravitational collapse and an outpouring of radiative energy. When such colossal forces finally balance, there is a burning in a state of steadiness, a meeting of hellish energy, so that even the greatest of stars burn for billions and billions of years; and even a small star, like our own sun, calmly consumes four billion tons of matter every second and does so for tens of billions of years. It is energy beyond comprehension, and yet it is a fragile and delicate balance.

So the fire could not burn. What raged in Cumberland, surrounded by warm and beautiful hills, was totally and utterly impossible. It was mad. It could not be, it could not exist.

It was a star no larger than the sharp point of a pin, it burned with a hundred million degrees, and it was beginning to twist and distort time and space in its immediate vicinity.

It did not run amuck because it was contained in a magic bottle made by man—a bottle with no physical form, but made up of energy, of woven electromagnetic force, a matrix of glowing force.

The delicate balance held—for now.

The star would not wane. Therefore, it must grow, and it would grow—although no one understood how it could even exist, let alone grow—in a cage of finite size.

It was more than a star. It was a nightmare where darkness was not permitted, a nightmare of the purest essence of light.

Star Bright.

4

Again, agents appeared at Owen Kimberly's home, at night, but they were not from NSA. They were FBI agents out of Denver, and their orders had come from the director of the Bureau, in a personally worded conversation. It had been made very clear that the orders had come from the president of the United States and were to be carried out to the letter, with no delay permitted.

There were more than twenty men, none of them aware of the why behind their assignment, but convinced that it was critical and imperative. They only knew that the man they had to bring to the White House was to be handled as if every ounce of fluid in his body were composed of nitroglycerin.

Jack Seidman had the detail. He was a big, powerful man devoted to his work and fully sensitive to the subtleties of the moment, as well as to the necessities. By the time he left Denver for St. Cloud, the machinery was well in motion. The

entire neighborhood about 28 Waverly Drive was
cordoned off, and all traffic was halted. The Colorado highway patrol, the county sheriff's department, and the St. Cloud police had all received
calls from the director of the FBI. Everyone understood, without it specifically being mentioned,
that the calls had been commanded by the president. Thus, no one was surprised when the cam-
pus grounds two miles from the home of Professor
Owen Kimberly were illuminated by several vehicles and a large military helicopter descended to
the grounds. Jack Seidman stepped out and along
with several other men raced off to confront the
man the president wanted before him.

Owen Kimberly, hardly surprised by the second
visit, was fully clothed when Jack Seidman appeared in his doorway. "What happened to Harlan?" he asked. "I'd have bet a nickel he wouldn't
have passed up the orders to bring me to Washington no matter what."

"I'm sorry, sir," Seidman replied in a heavy
rumble. "My orders are not to withhold any information from you. But all I know is that I am to
bring you to the office of President Whiteson without delay. I hope you'll cooperate, sir."

Kimberly studied the other man. "That's all you
know?"

"Yes, sir. My word."

Kimberly nodded. Seidman's presence told him
much. Tom Harlan had returned to Washington
where Adrian Russel at NSA had probably listened
with mingled disbelief and anger. Then, somehow
the president had been brought directly into the
stream of events. Therefore, there had been no
time for Harlan personally to return to St. Cloud.

The full effect of federal power was being exer-
cised. It didn't matter what agency was involved,
but at least they'd had the common sense not to
show up with men in uniform, for God's sake. So
Jack Seidman was only doing his job and with all
the courtesy, honestly presented, he could offer.

"I'll pack a few things," Kimberly said to the
FBI man.

"If you won't mind, sir, I'll go along. With another man," Seidman added. He saw the look on
Kimberly's face. "I apologize, professor. My orders are that once I have you in sight I am never
to let you out of—"

"Even if I have to go to the bathroom?"

No smile showed on Seidman's face. "Yes, sir.
The bathroom or anywhere else."

"All right. Come along, then."

The huge dog sensed something wrong and rose
to his feet, his hair bristling. On Kimberly's sharp
command, he sank slowly back to the floor. Then
the professor called the dog to follow him, reasoning that the animal would respond better if he
remained in his presence.

As he packed in his bedroom, Kimberly tried to
sort things through his mind. He should have
been a bit more orderly about this. He had known
that they'd be back, yet still they had caught him
off balance. He closed the zipper on his bag, and
before he could lift it from his bed, an FBI man had
it by the handle.

Kimberly looked from the dog to Seidman. "I'll
have to get someone to take care of him," he said.

"We'll handle everything, sir," Seidman said
quickly.

"No, you won't," Kimberly retorted. The urbanity of it all nettled him. "Unless this dog knows the person who attends him, he won't eat, and there's every chance he'll attack." His hand scratched behind a furry ear. "I won't permit that, of course. Besides, there's my fiancée. I must see her before I leave."

He nodded to himself. "Of course. She can handle Thor. He'll be good company for—"

"Professor, there isn't time for all that. We've got—"

"There *is* time, Mr. Seidman."

Jack Seidman gestured. "I'm really sorry, sir, but—"

"Do you want to have to knock me unconscious or fight both myself and this animal? Because you'll have to do that, Mr. Seidman. Do you understand me? I'm aware you're following your orders, but my wedding day is—or was supposed to be— *tomorrow*. Not too many hours from now, in fact." Kimberly drew himself up straighter. "We'll play a pleasant game, Mr. Seidman, but I do not leave here until this animal is with Angela and I say goodbye to her personally and explain why she's not getting married tomorrow." His brow furrowed as he added, "or perhaps ever."

The FBI agent looked puzzled, and Kimberly recognized his confusion. "You don't understand, of course, but suddenly I don't want to hear another word about your orders or security or what the president wants or anything else. Human values right now are the most important things in the world to me, and I'll not leave a vacuum behind me. So unless you're prepared to kill this dog and carry me out of here unconscious, you will cooperate with me."

Jack Seidman never missed a beat. "Yes, sir. Where does she live?"

"Her name is Angela Dobson, and she lives on Crescent Place, about a half-mile from here. I'll call her so we won't frighten her half to death. Is that all right with you?"

"Yes, sir."

Kimberly made the call to Angela, who listened with that incredible instant communication she had with him, understanding more than all his words might say. Minutes later the two agents, Kimberly, and the dog were in Angela's living room.

Kimberly held Angela very tightly, as he tried to explain why they could not be married that next morning and why two men stood watching everything he did. Kimberly's heart began pounding suddenly at the thought of leaving Angela behind. She was an auburn-haired woman, not beautiful in the classical sense, but with a face that an artist might describe as handsome. But to Owen Kimberly, Angela was beautiful in every sense and in every way, and his love for her was deep and meaningful. More, he knew her needs and his ability to fulfill what had been torn from her life. Three years before, her husband had died in the shattering crash of an airliner, leaving Angela with two small children to raise. Peter was now seven, and Susan had just passed her fourth birthday.

Angela filled as deep a void in Owen Kimberly's life as he filled in hers. He had never been married, had never had children. They had met at St. Cloud University, where they both taught. A quiet but responsive chord was struck, and they let their lives drift together. He was as crazy about the children as they were about him, and . . .

And now it was all being torn apart. Yet strangely, his own personal loss, as he held Angela, seemed to be drifting from him, as if he were becoming disembodied from his own life-form, his life, hers, and the intertwining that was soon to have joined them in marriage. Something tugged at Owen Kimberly—he did not know what it was—with an insistence far out of proportion to whatever reality he knew.

Angela sensed his loss of balance, his groping without knowing the reason, and she clung to him in one final embrace, kissed him strongly, then pulled away to hold him at arm's length. "You must go. No more explanations, Owen."

He nodded. He glanced at the dog lying on the rug nearby. "Stay," he said, and reached over, giving the animal a final brisk pat.

He turned back to Angela. "I don't know how long it will be, or—"

"I understand, Owen."

"No, no," he said quickly, almost fiercely. "If I have to be away for a while, I'll send for you and the children."

She fought back her desire to touch his face gently. "I love you. Now, go."

5

President Arthur Whiteson and Professor Owen Kimberly sat together in what could have been called a private den within the multitude of rooms, large and small, that made up the White House. The president used this room primarily as a retreat where he might recapture his senses when the pressures of his office stripped away his equilibrium. A fireplace glowed steadily, its gas-fed flames licking at "logs" that never burned. Even though it was artificial, the fireplace gave the room a measure of warmth that pleased Whiteson. This den was also a place where Whiteson felt comfortable in his pajamas and a robe, which is how he had greeted Professor Owen Kimberly. The president's attire had not been chosen only for comfort, however; it had calculatedly been worn to set Kimberly at ease. Whiteson knew that Kimberly had been hauled away from his own comforts, home, and security, and Whiteson had anticipated—correctly, he judged on meeting the man—that the trappings of office and an insistence on proper attire at four-thirty in the morning would have been a waste.

At six feet four inches, the president was almost the exact height of Owen Kimberly, and this gave them a physical comfort both men recognized without comment.

Owen Kimberly was more than pleased with his first impressions of the man who until this moment he had known only as a distant political figure, a face in print and animated only from the television screen—which Kimberly watched all too infrequently to have drawn lasting conclusions about the president of the country. Kimberly knew, however, that Whiteson was a brilliant politician and a skilled administrator. Kimberly's immediate judgment was that the president was a man of great life and vitality, shrewd and capable, who had brought into his office, with whatever else it had taken him to reach this dominant position, a measure of common sense not seen in the White House since the days when Harry S. Truman had salted the air with his own brand of pungency.

As they studied one another in their opening moments, Kimberly recalled that Whiteson was known to make instant decisions on which he stood, no matter in what direction the splinters flew. Originally he had achieved a great rapport with the Russians because they felt Whiteson was a man who understood the peculiarities of their system, who understood their now-enormous missile and nuclear strength, and who could also be pushed to whatever limit the Russians desired. However, a rambunctious performance on the part of the Soviet Union had brought on surprising responses in strength from Whiteson, as well as unexpected thrusts by the United States in different parts of the world, and the Soviet premier recognized that the United States president was a political chess player of unpredictable skill.

Owen Kimberly tried to recall what he had read about the president's private life. He remembered that Whiteson had been widowed for nearly eight years and that his children, all grown and imbued with the independence so savored by their father, were either in schools or in work of their own choosing in different parts of the world.

Owen Kimberly drew a pipe from his jacket. He smoked infrequently but suddenly felt the need, the physical actions of tamping the bowl and lighting up a measure of his own need to tranquilize his own racing thoughts. He was aware that he and the president had spent enough time sizing each other up, that they must now deal with the events that had brought them together.

"How familiar are you with the Cumberland operation?" began the president. "Oh, not the theory, Kimberly. The hard realities of what has happened down there."

"In its most succinct form—"

Arthur Whiteson smiled. "Thank you. I had hoped you knew how to cut the mustard. Forgive me."

Kimberly's response was warm. "I understand. I won't waste time or words. I know, from the press and my own knowledge of the project, that we've succeeded in igniting a thermonuclear flame and are containing the energy in what could roughly be called a force field—the magnetic sheath."

Arthur Whiteson studied him with great care. "And?"

"The rest, Mr. President, is deduction. Not in the scientific sense, but from"—and he gestured to take in his surroundings—"where I am right now and the events leading up to this moment. I might have been here sooner, but Adrian Russel—" He shrugged. "Well, sometimes he goes about things in the worst of all possible ways."

Whiteson shifted in his chair. "A personal matter?"

"No, no, not at all. My conclusions until a few hours ago were that Project Star Bright was in trouble—problems in the scientific or engineering sense, a technical matter. I must say I wasn't impressed with—"

"Nor concerned?"

"No, sir. It all came out as removing someone's chestnuts from a fire. Larry Pound is a good man behind a desk, but he's not a fireman, and it all sounded as if you've had—strictly in the metaphorical sense—a nasty fire on your hands."

Whiteson repressed a smile. It might have come out as a grimace of pain. "What's your conclusion right now, Kimberly?"

"I'm doing my best not to draw conclusions from insufficient information. Obviously something is *very* wrong. You are hardly the man, sir, to engage in such visits without compelling reason."

Whiteson snorted, an external sign of angry personal thoughts. "Kimberly, why the hell haven't you run this project?"

"Star Bright?" It was Kimberly's turn to withhold a grimace. "It's a long story, Mr. President, and I don't believe this is the time or the place."

"You may be wrong about that. You care to offer any theories as to why you're here? Beyond the obvious, I mean."

"I've been out of the business for a long time. So any conclusions, at least my own, need to rest on what is more than likely obsolescence."

"You were right when you answered before." President Whiteson studied the back of his hand. "They were quite successful in lighting their fire."

"Even that needs to be amplified. Mr. President, I'm not trying to be difficult. I may sound obtuse, or even ponderous, but it's not deliberate. There are all sorts of ways to—"

"I understand, Kimberly," the president broke in with a sudden gesture. "You know the route they went?"

Kimberly nodded. "The laser implosion system. Theoretically it's always been the way to go."

Whiteson met his gaze. "It works."

"So I understand from the reports I've seen."

"They got it all. Full ignition, full implosion. The works. Fusion like we've always dreamed of."

Kimberly frowned. This man was leading him somewhere, but he didn't know where. He had nothing else to say, so he said, "Yes, sir."

"But they can't put it out."

The realization of the enormity of the problem came to him so quickly, so quietly, that Owen Kimberly's immediate reflex was to blink his eyes rapidly several times, a sort of optic pause while his brain struggled to grasp the enormity of what he had just heard. The president studied the scientist before him, and he did not like what he saw. Owen Kimberly was a knowing and sensitive

man, as well as a figure of strength, and those few
words had struck him with devastating impact.

"For Christ's sake, man," Whiteson prodded
impatiently. "Say something."

"My God."

"Is that *all?*"

"Would it help if I threw up? I feel like it."
Kimberly nodded. "The laser implosion system.
the arms, the knuckles of his hands dead white. "I
mean, my God"—a wan smile appeared on his
face—"I don't believe you. Do you understand
what I mean?" Kimberly's face showed an expression of almost pleading. "I mean, I don't *want* to
believe you!"

Arthur Whiteson had just watched his worst
fears materialize in the reaction of this man to his
words. "Is it that bad, then?"

Kimberly was half out of his chair. "What the
hell do you mean," he asked loudly, "they can't
put it out?"

"They ignited the fire. They got implosion with
cryogenic pellets, they got fusion, and when they
got fusion, instead of an energy burst, they got a
very clean, very intense fire."

"A fusion fire?"

"That's right, Professor."

"That is *still* burning?"

"It won't go out. They don't know how to put it
out. They've tried."

"They might as well have used water to put out
the sun!"

"You are not an encouraging person, Professor."

"I am a frightened man, Mr. President." He
screwed up his face as he racked his memory for
things long committed to some cerebral dead-file,

and when he pulled the wisps of memory cards from their slots, the feeling of dread he had first experienced kept growing in him. He looked up again at the president. "There's no doubt—I mean that—"

The president sighed. "There's no question."

"Then it could be worse than—" Kimberly shook his head. "We don't have words for how bad it could be. Sir, Dr. Clayton is the chief scientist on this project. May I recommend that I be able to talk with him as soon as possible?"

Whiteson rose to his feet and slowly crossed the room. He stood before the fireplace, staring into the curling flames. The warmth touched softly at his skin. "He's here in the White House. Along with his assistant, Kathy Farral, and Dr. Lawrence Pound."

Behind the president, Kimberly was also on his feet. "I need to talk with him at once." The professor was astonished at his assertiveness with the president, but something had sliced through whatever protocol or political or personal awe he should have felt with the man who ran the country and dictated which way the world might move in its political orbit. That was all, suddenly, nonsense.

"I'll take care of it," Whiteson said, turning suddenly. "Thirty minutes from now. Why don't you take the time to wash up and meet me back here then? One of my aides will show you to your room and return you here." He smiled crookedly. "I may as well get dressed myself. I doubt very much if I'll be doing any more sleeping for a while."

*   *   *

For the first time in many years, Owen Kimberly faced Dick Clayton. "You look good," Kimberly genially said to the man who had been only a laboratory assistant the last time they had met and who had since made use of the glittering foundation of knowledge he, Owen Kimberly, had laid down.

But Clayton failed to respond in kind. He was formal to the point of awkward stiffness as he shook hands with Kimberly.

Dr. Richard Clayton, judged Owen Kimberly, seemed a man clinging desperately to reality—which threatened to shake him loose and blow him away in the dusty winds of the past.

"Professor Kimberly," Clayton said, nodding slightly.

An attractive woman—and any woman who could seem attractive at this ungodly hour of the day had to be something special, Kimberly thought—edged closer. "Professor, I'm Kathy Farrel, Dr. Clayton's assistant. I've looked forward to meeting you for a long time."

Kimberly returned her warm greetings. The dark-haired woman immediately impressed him. Clayton looked as if he'd been shattered—although with good reason—by what was happening down at Cumberland, yet this woman who assisted him somehow retained her sense of ease and perspective. That was good. Reliability under crushing stress wasn't all that common, and Kimberly formed an immediate opinion that this woman was likely to prove the kind of bedrock they would all need.

"Where's Dr. Pound?" Kimberly asked.

Richard Clayton's hands fidgeted along the back of a chair. "He— uh—won't be with us."

"Something wrong with him?" They turned at the sound of President Whiteson's voice; he had come into the room just in time to hear the question and its response.

Clayton turned, startled. He took a deep breath and let it out suddenly. *The man's nearly a wreck,* Kimberly thought.

"Uh, no, sir, it's just that he—uh—took a sedative before he went to bed," Clayton said, his words and manner staccato. "He wouldn't be able to—I mean—"

Whiteson's sudden gesture dismissed the subject of Dr. Lawrence Pound. "It's all right, Clayton," the president interjected. "Administration isn't what we need right now."

He sat down in the same chair he had occupied when he had been alone with Kimberly and waited until the others were seated. Then he spoke.

"I don't want any preambles or background," he said, and Kimberly noted his voice had taken on a measure of hardness that had been absent only a half-hour before. "Dr. Clayton, you will bring Professor Kimberly up to date, in a tight and orderly progression of events. Doctor Farrel, you're free to interrupt to add whatever you feel is necessary. Professor Kimberly, if there are points that need clarification, please break in at those moments. If any of you feel that what you are saying regarding technical matters is over my head, continue as you are. I can always ask my own questions later, as I may do at any time. For the record, this entire conversation is being taped, and transcripts will be prepared immediately afterward. Now, Dr. Clayton, if you will, please."

There was a solid forty-five minutes of technical exchange between the two men. President Arthur Whiteson didn't make the mistake of trying to comprehend the deeper physics, but was content for the moment to catch critical phrases and above all to study the two men and the woman. For those forty-five minutes, he listened to a wealth of questions and answers, of angry statements and retorts on each side, and from it all the president extracted nuances and conclusions he knew he would need for his own guidance later.

There was a decided shift in how the exchange went. For a time Professor Owen Kimberly remained content to ask questions, to probe and sift so he might update himself on the ramifications of advancements in technical and industrial processes. Then steadily and unmistakably, as he gathered the information he needed, Owen Kimberly went onto what could only be described as an offensive. His questions came faster and faster until he seemed the schoolmaster drilling a brilliant but incomplete student. The swift firing of questions shifted slowly to accusing looks, then sharp tones, and finally, condemnation. As Whiteson leaned forward, Kimberly accused the director of Star Bright of "stark, raving incompetence."

President Whiteson knew it was time to break in. They were at the crux of the matter. "Kimberly, just a moment."

The professor drew up short, almost biting his tongue. He leaned back in his chair and turned to the president. His face was white, his cheek muscles knotted. "Yes, sir," he said slowly.

Whiteson realized that Kimberly had been on

the thin edge of hurling himself at Clayton and battering the man with his great fists.

"Professor Kimberly, are you accusing Dr. Clayton, and those who work with him, of a major error in their calculations?" The president hated sounding pedantic, but he had to maneuver emotions as well as the incredible brainpower in the room with him.

"Accusing? No!" Kimberly shouted. "There's no accusation to make!" He turned in his chair, anger and shock stamped indelibly on his face. Whiteson glanced at Clayton. The man was almost trembling.

"It's not a matter of accusing," Kimberly said, taking long and shuddering breaths. "It's what they've *done*, what's going on at this very instant. Mr. President, the only way I can say this to you is that any danger we have ever faced, as a nation and as a planet, is meaningless compared to what is happening right now."

He flung his arm out, stabbing the air in the direction of Richard Clayton and Kathy Farrel. "You fools. You bloody fools. Stupid, bungling idiots—"

"That's enough." Whiteson's voice had the right measure of sharpness to bring the beginning of the explosive tirade to a halt. He had found the clue, the word.

"Professor Kimberly, you used the term 'bungling.' Are you referring to something specific? Be clear, please."

Again Kimberly took a long, deep breath in an attempt to calm himself. "Yes, sir," he said, forcing himself to slow his words. "There has always been a single critical danger point in commencing steady fusion. It's a matter that—"

"No one could have foreseen—" At Kimberly's angry glance, Clayton's interruption trailed off.

Kimberly went on. "The danger point is that we're dealing with much that is unknown. So every fusion ignition test must have, we'll call it a blowout, a safety valve for a better word, to immediately get rid of accumulating energy. It's like a bomb explosion, Mr. President. The moment the energy release goes beyond a certain point, you let it blow. Deliberately. You get a controlled explosion that way, and you're keeping pressures from building up to where you *can't* control them. All this is an oversimplification, of course, and—"

"It will do fine. Continue," the president said quickly.

"When the fusion fire was ignited, there was always a danger of something unforeseen happening. So the only way to play it safe was to have the magnetic sheath—the bottle of force—have what we call a blow-out level. That's the safety valve. If the energy built too fast to control, then the bottle would collapse. You would have an explosion on your hands, but you'd know basically what you were getting. If you make your tests in an underground chamber, and it's sealed off—well, sir, we explode hydrogen bombs underground in complete safety."

The look on his face as he studied Dr. Richard Clayton was one of mingled anger and contempt. "They didn't do that. They were so eager to have success on their hands that they tested their fusion ignition in a building—*above the ground*. That is so stupid as to be criminal, because—as one step follows another—to protect themselves and the immediate area, they built the magnetic bottle, the container, of such strength that it *wouldn't* blow."

Kimberly looked directly at the president. "The container is holding. For now. But what they have inside that force bottle is an incredible creature of pure energy that quite possibly may be getting stronger with every passing moment, and when it does blow, its force will be incalculable." Kimberly shook his head. "I don't know all this for certain. But what I do know is that we're tampering with the same energy that makes the stars we see in the sky. The smallest error could be utterly catastrophic."

He turned to look directly at Richard Clayton. "Didn't you at least read what I wrote about years ago? It's all there in black and white! My calculations, the dangers. My God, man, all you needed to do was a computer study of the energy potential, and all this could have been avoided. I—"

He went silent for a moment, and no one broke into the sudden quiet. Finally he came to the question he had asked before and knew he must voice again. "Clayton, tell me once more. It burns in a steady state? No fluctuation, no change?"

"As far as we can tell," Clayton responded in a strained voice.

"What does that mean?" the president asked.

"It's impossible." Kimberly's reply was flat and unequivocal.

"It's impossible, but it's happening?"

"Yes."

"Marvelous," the president murmured. He looked at the three people with him—Kimberly a bundle of barely controlled rage, Clayton hanging on as tightly as he could to his own self-control, the woman quietly in control of herself. Time to fish or cut bait, thought Arthur Whiteson.

"What do you recommend?" he asked Kimberly.

"I want these people to return at once to Cumberland, Mr. President, so they can begin to make the computer studies of what we've discussed in this room and establish a line of possibilities with which we can work. We need to get a handle on what's happening, to see if there's any shift or change. Once we have that, even the slightest alteration can give us a hint of where to go. I want them to do that and get that information to me at once. I don't know," he added slowly. "Perhaps I ought to be there myself. I—"

"Not yet, not yet, Kimberly." Whiteson turned to Clayton and Farrel. "Do you two agree with what Professor Kimberly has recommended?"

Clayton nodded slowly, but Kathy Farrel's answer was clear. "Yes, sir. It's the only thing to do."

"Forgive me for being abrupt, then," Whiteson said, rising to his feet. "I want you to leave immediately. My aide will have you flown directly from Washington to Cumberland. Dr. Pound, of course, is to accompany you. Whatever you find that may be of *any* value is to be communicated at once, no matter what time of day or night, to myself or to Professor Kimberly. You will have priority in reaching me."

The president touched a button on his armchair. "Colonel Ledbetter, you have all this?"

A voice came from a wall speaker. "Yes, sir. We'll attend to it at once."

The door opened at the same time, and an aide

stood waiting for Clayton and Farrel. They said their goodbyes quickly and left.

Then the president was alone again with Kimberly. "You'll have to lay it out to me again," he told the scientist. "How bad this thing is, how bad it may get, the best we can hope for and the worst we may expect. Another point occurs to me—do you mind if I call you Owen? Good. The point of time. How much of it do we have? You have been very strong in references to a time limit in all this, and that seems to me to be the essential factor in everything. What is there in your papers—how long ago was it?"

"Eleven years, sir."

"What was it you saw eleven years ago that frightens you so badly today?"

Kimberly's face had a measure of resignation, almost defeat, that displeased Whiteson. "It's all in my papers," he started. "I—"

Whiteson gestured impatiently. "Don't give me a lecture. *Tell* me, man."

6

"There's no other way, sir. I apologize if it seems as if I'm talking down to you," Kimberly said with care, "but you *need* a capsule lecture if all this is going to make sense."

"I was afraid of that," admitted Whiteson. "Don't apologize. I'm aware of the essentials of fusion. Energy has been a prime consideration of this office ever since I've been in here. But I'm a politician first and an understanding layman a very poor second. Have at it, Owen."

"Yes, sir. I want to stress again that without a grounding in the subject, I'm afraid you might miss certain critical junctures, and not appreciate the terrible urgency I'm trying to impress upon you."

The president let out a long sigh, almost a groan. "You make me feel as if I'm back in college," he complained lightly. He went across the room to open a cabinet bar and mixed drinks for them both. After giving Owen his, the president sat down again in his chair, removed his shoes, and kneaded the muscles of his feet.

"All right, Professor, go ahead."

Kimberly took a long swallow, held the glass in both hands, and stared into it. "Sir, just how familiar are you with thermonuclear fusion? We could cut time—"

"Let's say, Owen, that I'm not unfamiliar with it. Like I said, energy resources and research has been a major plank with me. I have to know something about the subject. Obviously," he said drily, "the need for energy is there. People are scared to death of atomic reactors, especially the breeder plants with dangers of leakage and explosions and producing weapons-grade plutonium. Well, you know all that. But I have a scientific board that's on my neck every week. I have a nation that's howling for energy, for today, for tomorrow, for the years ahead. So I've got to know something about the subject. I also need to combine it with everything else in running this country so that—" He ended his words with a thin smile. "It's your platform, Professor. Go on."

"I'm going to have to be personal to some extent." Kimberly paused, but the president gestured him to continue. "Were you aware, sir, that Star Bright was the name I gave, many years ago, to a theoretical program for fusion?"

"No, I wasn't."

Kimberly held his words for the moment, for his mind had insisted on drifting away, trying to find its own perspective. He had a sudden, stinging impression of Angela, and thought again that this was to be his day of marriage, and here he was, seated in the White House. Somehow, at this moment, he found it impossible to separate his thoughts of the woman he loved from the terrible thing burning in the heart of the Cumberland hills. Damn it, he wanted his explanation to be clear and specific, but he was torn with his own thoughts—including the thoughts of what had happened to him personally. They wouldn't leave him, but tugged inside his mind, demanding their moment of attention.

He had long believed the old bitterness to have fled, for Kimberly had come to cherish the scholastic honors he received from students and faculty, recognizing him as an individual they held in great respect. The warmth, yes, even the love he had found in St. Cloud had slowly but effectively erased the rejection and back-stabbing he had endured years before when nuclear science and the promise of fusion power had lured him to government laboratories. Then, younger and brash, he had reacted to his co-workers' pettiness and their struggle for political power rather than scientific truth with harsh statements and brazen condemnation of his peers and his official superiors.

The results were predictable. It didn't matter that Kimberly was the most brilliant and promising scientist to come along in years, nor did it matter that he had an incredible understanding of thermonuclear reactions that could well lead the way to discovering vast amounts of energy for a nation feeding voraciously on such energy. You do not buck the system, he was told.

You join the team.

"Get on the stick," his immediate superior had told him, but doing so meant subordinating his own genius to bureaucratic mediocrity. Kimberly rebelled. The government reacted predictably. They threw Kimberly out.

But they had kept everything he had learned, prepared, and theorized, because he had been on a government contract and those were the terms of his employment.

Well, he had reacted as well. He was fed to the teeth with being called an obstructionist only because he refused to set his pace with men too far behind his own work to understand what he pushed. He did not have the thick skin of the experienced researcher who threads the maze of governmental research, so he totally rejected the federally sponsored scientific community. He was as much a maverick as he was a genius, and individuality won out. Kimberly abandoned the field of theoretical research and took a position as instructor in the remote small college of St. Cloud in Colorado.

His security clearance had been revoked, and he made no effort to reinstate this key to continued access to "inside" progress in fusion power. He cloaked himself in the obscurity of a small educational community, and he found a peace that he had never dreamed existed. Rapport with his students came swiftly and across deep levels, for in this time and age scholastic rebellion and individuality were marks to be sought, and Professor Owen Kimberly was a separatist supreme. Students fought to get into his classes. The man transformed science into a glowing and visible wonder. Physics became a reality, the numbing demands of higher mathematics became an enchanted loom, and the world was alive.

For a while, his past faded, and he settled into a comfortable niche. But then he began to read in scientific journals that scientists were about to bring a long-existent project to reality—they were attempting to create the fusion fire that burned in a star. He was unprepared for the excitement he felt as he read the articles.

Star Bright, they called it. *His name*. He detested the bitterness the old memories stirred up in him. But he could hardly prevent the siren call of reading everything on the subject; not to do so would have been a rejection of the seeker in his own mind.

And they did it—it was the end product of thirty years of hammering struggle, three decades of impossible scientific research and staggering engineering feats come true. Thirty years and thirty billion dollars and worth every damned year and every dollar, and—

"You've been somewhere, Owen."

The president's voice jolted him from his memories.

"I'm sorry," he apologized. "I was trying to put it all together. You know, the personal and the scientific. I was also thinking about how I came up with the name of Star Bright. I created the name in a moment of poetic whimsy. Man reaching into the heart of a star to snatch the fire that writhes and boils within. Maybe the myth about Prometheus had some real truth to it," he said ruefully. "Perhaps men weren't—aren't—ready to be given the fire made for the gods. Prometheus may have earned his comeuppance."

Whiteson smiled with the thought of it. "I almost regret forcing you back to the mundane. But our world is of men and not gods."

"Yes, sir. There were some other things I was

thinking about. I've been trying to understand the compulsion behind what Clayton and the others have been doing."

"And have you?" Whiteson had a trace of a smile on his face.

"Perhaps," Kimberly said, answering carefully. "I *am* trying to see things from their point of view because maybe I can understand better what happened—what's happening right now—down in Tennessee. Power, any kind of power, is terribly compelling and—" He cut himself short and couldn't avoid the burst of laughter at his own words. The president understood; it was strange to be telling the man who could launch twenty thousand hydrogen bombs against the world about power.

Kimberly went on with sudden sobriety. "You see, sir, the way Clayton and the others must look at this whole thing, soaring to the moon with Apollo has to be a side issue compared to fusion power. Even building the atomic bomb back in 1945 was a slingshot affair. Nothing man has ever done can compare to limitless energy, for it can change the world to an extent beyond our imagination. For the good, I would hope. A world where energy is cheap and available everywhere. It would mean industrial, agricultural, scientific plenitude—"

"I want to ask you again if you consider all this relevant," Whiteson chided him gently.

Kimberly pushed his fingers through his hair. "I don't know," he said honestly. "I think it is. At least it's helping me find my own way through the thickets. If you want me to stay closer to the hard nut of all this, Mr. President, I will do—"

"No, no. By all means thread your path, Owen.

You're right; you may find answers we can't anticipate."

"Thank you, sir. You see, I was trying to link what we're doing with the history of getting where we are. For example, through what we call modern history, man has hacked his way through progressive ages. Each one has been a highwater mark in his social and scientific evolution. We've been through the ages of stone, fire, metal, industry, flight—those and many more. But all of it led up to the eight years of the Second World War, from 1937 into 1945. When we came out of that war, we had been hurled—and hurled is the word for it, because it was a quantum jump in knowledge and capability—into something for which we were totally unprepared.

"We were exploding our way into the future. We did this by plunging into several ages concurrently, rushing ahead along what were parallel *and* intertwining streams."

"You make it sound rather furious," murmured Whiteson.

"It is, and it will be more so," Kimberly responded. "Suddenly man was in the midst of the jet, atomic, and space ages, as well as the one age that made all these possible, the computer age. They all came at once, and we were drowning in it. We're barely treading water right now because the one age we failed to anticipate that absolutely had to emerge from all the others was the—"

"Let's call it the energy crunch," the president interrupted. "It seems more fitting than the age of energy," he observed. "If anything, it's the *lack* of energy that's hit us so hard."

"Yes, sir, and that's as well said as if the words

were my own," Kimberly told him. He was unaware of how pleased Arthur Whiteson was to hear his remark, for if Kimberly held the president in awe, the feeling was reciprocated fully. "Well," Kimberly went on, "you know the rest—how we built our massive dams and power plants, tamed rivers, sucked petroleum from the crust of the planet; all of it. We built our atomic bombs, and we gloried in our computers. Men have rushed about their world on silvered wings and hurtled to the moon and come home safely. All our glorious visions have come real."

"And we have four billion people in the world today who—"

"Who are starving in every way for what energy, if it's available, can do for them," Kimberly finished.

"Let me interrupt this a moment. I want to jump ahead," Whiteson prodded. "We're running out of fossil fuels. We're gouging the planet for coal. Solar power simply can't meet the energy needs we have. Fuel cells are toys. Tidal basins and geothermal energy and *all* the plans aren't enough. What it all amounts to, Owen, is that if we want to keep the wheels of this world turning, we have to duplicate what goes on inside an average class-B star. Our sun."

"Yes, sir, except that it's impossible."

Whiteson raised his eyebrows. "But I thought that that is what we *had*," he offered in mild protest. "What's going on down in Cumberland? Isn't that a duplicate of the fusion process inside the sun?"

"No, sir, it isn't," Kimberly said, shaking his head slightly, his expression showing his need for patience on the part of his one-man audience. "It's not *quite* the same. The difference is small, but it's everything."

"Apparently more than I was aware," Whiteson said, obviously nettled.

"My apologies. I—"

"Not *you*, dammit, Owen. What's the difference?"

"Anytime you want to have the enormous energy from fusion you need two things: absolutely enormous temperatures and just as enormous density. The sun has that because it's an immense body with a staggering gravitational field. Every single second the sun fuses six hundred million tons of hydrogen into helium. I don't want to go into the equations—"

"Don't you dare. I couldn't stand it," Whiteson warned him.

"The heart of the matter is that the only reason the sun works as a fusion furnace is its incredible gravitational field. It's able to trap and keep caged the temperatures required for fusion. Well, we can't do that here on the earth. We don't have hydrogen at the densities that exist inside the sun, and when we do fuse a large amount of material we—"

"Have a hydrogen bomb on our hands."

"Exactly."

"I've heard it called gravitational confinement— the way the temperatures and densities are controlled within the sun. Is that right?"

"Yes, sir, it is. But there is absolutely no way we can create, here on earth, the gravitational fields of the sun. It would be a monstrous violation of all laws of physics."

"Then—"

"We have to work with even higher temperatures. Since we can't match the densities in the sun, we've got to create temperatures that are far greater."

"That seems equally impossible," Whiteson protested. "Look, you're talking—how high?"

"A hundred million degrees. Maybe more."

"It sounds like the universal solvent. It dissolves everything. So what the hell do you use to hold it in?"

"A perfect analogy. We couldn't hope to build a container that can hold a hundred million degrees, so we—"

Whiteson was nodding slowly. "Of course. If you can't do what's patently impossible you build—"

"The magnetic sheath. The magic bottle of electromagnetic forces. The force field. It can't contain those temperatures for very long. Just long enough."

"Owen, where do the lasers come in? I know we need laser beams to start the fire, but how?" Quickly he held up a hand. "And for God's sake, man, keep it simple."

"Yes, sir," Kimberly said. He didn't know whether to feel chastised or not, but he recognized the president's need for understanding without lecturing. Keep it simple, he ordered himself, just tell the dammed thing like it is.

"I'll take it step by step, Mr. President. The only way to get the fusion fire is by extreme temperature and the only way that this high temperature is useful is if it's confined long enough for us to draw off that heat and convert it to electrical energy."

"Tell me how."

"We create a vacuum chamber. Around this chamber we have a huge array of laser beams, and their energy levels are enormous. Thirty beams might be used to focus on a single spot smaller than a pinhead, so that we'd be dealing with maybe fifty million joules in a hundred picoseconds and—" Kimberly slowed to a stop at the look on the president's face, then he said hastily, "I should have explained first that a joule is one watt for one second, of course, and that a hundred picoseconds is a hundred trillionths of a second, and—"

"And nothing. Forget the crazy numbers, Owen! You have all your laser beams. You aim them at a tiny spot. *What happens?*"

"We drop a pellet into the chamber."

"What kind of pellet?"

"We call it D-T. It's made of deuterium-tritium, and—"

"*What* is it?"

"Essentially, supercold hydrogen, about a thousand times denser than normal hydrogen."

"How big is this pellet of yours?"

"You could put more than a hundred of them on the head of a pin."

Whiteson took that in silence. "All right. You drop this pellet into your chamber. The chamber, I assume, is surrounded by the magnetic bottle?"

"Yes, sir." Obviously the president was struggling through with his own questions, and Kimberly was more than glad to go along with this new line.

"Let's keep it one step at a time. You drop your pellet into the chamber, and it gets zapped by your laser beams. Is that right?"

"In a simplistic form, yes."

"Simplistic does me fine, Owen. Okay, your laser beams zap the pellet. What happens?"

"Several things—"

"One at a time, Owen, one at a time."

"Yes, sir. The laser beams compress the pellet."

"Keep going."

"They compress it to a density more than ten thousand times greater than before the laser beams—as you put it, sir—zapped the pellet."

"Owen, you said your supercold pellet was a thousand times denser than normal hydrogen?"

"Yes, sir."

"And now you're compressing it again by a factor of ten thousand?"

"Yes, sir."

"Your compression is on the order of ten million times normal, then."

"Yes, sir, it is."

"What happens next?"

"In just about a trillionth of a second, the temperature reaches a hundred million degrees."

"Which does what?"

"It causes fusion. Part of the hydrogen turns into helium."

"Presto," murmured Arthur Whiteson. "The hydrogen turns into helium. We've got fusion. And this does?"

"It creates a flood of fusion energy that's contained within the magnetic bottle."

"What happens to the energy, Owen?"

"The energy is converted to heat we can handle. Part of the chamber has what we call an energy converter. This has special types of materials. It uses the heat energy to evaporate a liquid—"

"Hold it right there. You've got a pellet small

enough for a hundred of them to fit onto the size of a pinhead. How much energy do you get when you compress—or zap, or whatever—that pellet with the laser beams? In a trillionth of a second, I believe you said?"

"Yes, sir. One pellet should produce, at the lowest level, the energy output of ten pounds of dynamite."

"So you've got a hellish blast in a confined chamber. It heats a liquid in some complicated system you people have put together. The liquid—"

"Not simply heated. It's evaporated," Kimberly corrected.

Whiteson nodded. "All right. It's evaporated. You transfer this heat?"

"Yes, sir."

"To what?"

"It drives generators that create electricity."

"Ordinary garden-variety electricity we can use for everyday purposes?"

"That's correct."

"If you want to keep the system going, you keep dropping in your pellets, keep zapping them, keep producing that energy?"

"Exactly."

"Professor Kimberly," the president sighed, "that has been the most incredible, roundabout conversation I have ever heard for describing what is essentially an internal combustion engine. The very same kind of engine that runs every automobile in this country."

Owen Kimberly sat with a stunned expression on his face. His mouth worked, but for several seconds he held back the words he started. "That's a tremendous oversimplification, sir, and I—"

"Owen, one and one equal two no matter how you add them up."

"No, sir, they don't."

Arthur Whiteson stared at this man who dealt with the energy of stars like other men build boats in their basement. Finally he sighed. "Do me a favor, Owen. Make yourself a drink. Make us both a drink. But don't say anything for a while. My head feels as if you've hit it with a few of those lasers of yours. Just let me sit here quietly and think, will you?"

Jesus Christ, all this time and a splitting headache, but it was worth it. He'd found what he was looking for. The crux of it all. *One and one do not equal two.* Wonderful, he thought sarcastically.

"Owen, make mine a double."

7

Much of what Professor Owen Kimberly had just said, President Whiteson already knew. But the man had a manner of presentation vastly different from anyone else with whom President Arthur Whiteson had discussed the subject. He was completely at ease, at home, as it were, with the fusion genie and the magic bottles of electromagnetic forces containing the creature struggling to get loose. Through Kimberly, the president hoped to slice through the mind-numbing complexities with which everyone else dealt with the subject. Kimberly had no idea that the president had already scanned his early reports and had read summations and opinions of what Kimberly had written and recommended so many years back. Not all of it, of course, but the vital gleanings.

Long before this moment, Kimberly had made his warnings ringingly explicit. There lay within the attempts to harness fusion energy certain critical unknowns. Because there were unknown forces, every experiment contained the danger of unleashing its own unpleasant gifts from some thermonuclear Pandora's box. Kimberly had stressed this point again and again, and he had thundered from his pulpit of equations the lessons that should have been learned from programming errors made during the preparations for the early tests of hydrogen bombs.

Years before this very night, scientists had tinkered with the awesome forces of fusion. On a Pacific Island far removed from prying eyes and secluded from the world, they had prepared to detonate an experimental device that was to yield the explosive force of two million tons of TNT. Not a really big bomb, anymore, as the thermonukes went, but in those days it was to the atomic bomb what that horrendous weapon had been to Hiroshima and Nagasaki. Two megatons. Easily controlled.

Kimberly was a lone voice in the early darkness of the thermonuclear age saying that the scientists were in error. There was a flaw in their calculations. The computers were wrong because the men who fed their calculations into the computer did so in error. Therefore the computer "lied." But Kimberly was young, brash, far down in the pecking order of scientists involved in the ultrasecret project, and security restrictions kept his voice tunneled and muted.

Kimberly was right—the bomb went off with a force of fifteen million tons. The scientists, however, were not upset; they were both delighted and bemused because they had vindicated their theories of weapons development as well as given the nation a hell of a lot more bang for the buck than had been appropriated. But then the test of a

five-megaton bomb—preceded in its ignition once
again by the now strident but still unheeded voice
of Owen Kimberly—ripped the Pacific atmosphere
with the terrifying blast of more than forty million
tons. No one knew for certain just how much more
than forty megatons had been released because
scientific instruments hadn't been prepared for such
a contingency. But the test island vanished, and
the sea bottom burned for three days and nights.

The next planned test was of a weapon designed
to yield fifty million tons of explosive force. By
then Owen Kimberly was nearly hysterical. He
went to the head of the Atomic Energy Commission and told him an X factor was present and that
the weapon had every chance of exploding in the
gigaton range—which meant an explosive yield of
billions of tons. The explosion could also produce
an atmosphere blowout and terrifying consequences
for the entire planet.

Shortly thereafter, the AEC released a brief
statement that all planned goals in weapons development had been attained and further tests of
"massive yield thermonuclear devices" were un-
necessary. No one, however, ever publicly admitted that Kimberly's calculations and his warnings
had affected the planned test or had anything to
do with its cancellation. But in reports prepared
by the National Security Agency, the Atomic Energy Commission, the Department of Defense, and
nearly every other weapon and scientific group of
the government, the name of Owen Kimberly
appeared—often buried in footnotes, but nevertheless there.

The step from weaponry to fusion power was
inevitable, and once again Owen Kimberly began

stirring his own cauldron of dissent. He had prepared a theoretical program of fusion power absolutely brilliant in its concept and crystal clear in its statements, and he warned that the same X factor that prevailed in the weapons tests could not be avoided in trying to control the energy of fusion. There were unprecedented effects that hovered on the edge of full-energy tests. Kimberly warned that any experiments should be made in deep underground chambers especially designed to absorb titanic explosions, that once a certain energy level was reached within the force field intended to contain that energy, it must be permitted to yield, to break down—in short, the uncontrolled explosion must be allowed to take place under conditions that would not result in catastrophe. But the scientists ignored his warnings and by the time the energy crisis hit, Owen Kimberly had been long gone from government research.

The nation needed energy, it clawed in every direction for energy. It damned the Arab bloc for its fiscal dice-rolling with the petroleum remains of dinosaurs long departed; it enforced publicly attentive but ineffective cutbacks in electrical consumption. The nation was on a wild roller coaster, and it needed electrical juice to keep going. The fusion program moved ahead with full force, and there grew within the ranks of scientists and project directors a fierce competition. The man who bulldozed *this* program through to success would be a national hero, an international figurehead, heaped with honors and able to write his own ticket for the rest of his life. That was an impetus infinitely more compelling than meeting stated project goals "for the good of all."

*   *   *

To President Arthur Whiteson, Owen Kimberly's
remarks represented the first scraping of the key
in the lock to what the hell was going on in Tennessee where the impossible had taken and was
still taking place. Whiteson was deft in screening
and filtering the facts he had been given. He knew
he was on the right track with Kimberly, but still
he had to poke and prod and lead the man along,
because only in this way could critical rapport be
achieved and could he crawl within Kimberly's
mind. There would be no time later, Whiteson
was convinced, and it must happen *now*.

Kimberly had, with the direction of the president, presented his prologue, his setting up of all
his calculations. The time for the nitty-gritty was
now, decided Whiteson, as he sipped at his drink.
He dragged them both back into the thermonuclear thickets.

"Owen, I'd like to ask some basic questions."

Owen Kimberly, his drink held untouched in
his hands, blinked several times. His mind had
been impossibly far away, in the midst of energies
he tried to comprehend but which he knew must
still lie beyond the mental reach of any human
mind. He drew himself up short. "Yes, sir."

"Owen, using what you called the D-T material,
the—"

"Deuterium-tritium."

"Right. Using this material, what's the energy
available to us?"

Kimberly was again at home. "Under full fusion,
one kilogram would—"

"That's 2.2 pounds, isn't it?"

"Yes, sir. One kilogram undergoing fusion would

yield to us an energy output of 100,000,000 kilowatthours."

Arthur Whiteson absorbed that fact quietly for a moment. "That's theoretical?"

"It's practical, Mr. President."

"All right. Let me get back to this magic bottle, this force field of ours. Forget for the moment what I may or may not know about it or what you've already told me. I want you to guide me carefully."

"Of course."

"Why do we need the force field? This magnetic bottle?"

"Well, it's easy enough, Mr. President. Nothing physical, that is, nothing we could build out of any materials we know, could endure a temperature higher than six thousand degrees."

"But you *do* have a physical structure of some kind for the fusion process, don't you?"

"Oh, yes, sir, we have to have that. This is the vacuum chamber, and the force field is created *inside* the chamber. You see, any time you create a gas in a chamber, and you expose that gas to an electrical charge—to a discharge, really—the gas is broken up. When we implode the D-T pellet and create our high temperatures, we're converting the material of the pellet into a gas. It explodes or boils outward at a speed of a thousand miles a second. The trick here, Mr. President, is to keep the tremendous effect of that gas—we also call the gas a plasma; it's a more accurate representation—from striking the walls of the vacuum chamber."

Whiteson held up his hand. "Try to keep it simple enough for me to understand, please."

Owen Kimberly gave the other man a crooked

grin. "I've been getting the idea that through most of this, you've been slightly ahead of me, Mr. President."

"Don't be so sure," Whiteson responded smoothly. "I'm after something, I believe you're the only man to give it to me, and I *need* to follow this route. Now, you were saying—?"

"Well, think of this cloud of plasma, boiling away from the D-T pellet as it's struck by the laser beams. It moves out at a thousand miles a second, and we've got to keep it from striking the walls of our chamber, or it would destroy it in an instant. We feed a constant electrical discharge into the chamber. This takes the electrified gas, the plasma, and breaks it up into its electrically charged components, such as protons or electrons—"

"Into what we'd call ions," the president offered.

"Precisely. Now, we can control the plasma stream because anything of this nature can be controlled by magnetic force fields—or lines of force; it comes out to the same thing. We sustain very powerful magnetic fields throughout the vacuum chamber. The magnetic force field makes up what we call the bottle, and—"

"Let me try that one. Your plasma now travels along the lines of magnetic force. So it's really whirling around with tremendous speed *inside* the vacuum chamber but never touching its walls. In effect it's a confined force field *within* the chamber. Then, you're able to use the tremendous heat of that plasma to evaporate the liquid of your heat converter and use it to generate electrical power?"

Owen Kimberly looked carefully at the man in the easy chair. Despite everything that had been said, President Arthur Whiteson had needed no guidance through the pathway they had traveled. He seemed to be seeking confirmation for, or trying to group together, his own thoughts. Finally Kimberly nodded. "Yes, sir, that's just the way the system works."

Whiteson sipped at his drink. "Let me go back for a moment to those tiny pellets you're dropping into the vacuum chamber. I want to be absolutely certain of something. You said you could fit a hundred of these, perhaps more, onto the head of a single pin?"

"Yes, sir."

"And the implosion by laser beam of one such pellet releases energy equal to the explosion of ten pounds of dynamite."

"That's correct."

"Now, Owen, what's the rate at which you feed these pellets into the vacuum chamber?"

"In a full-size operating system, we would detonate about one hundred pellets per second."

Whiteson didn't even hesitate. "That's a ton of explosive energy in a confined space every two seconds."

Kimberly nodded. "You can see the scale of progression, of course."

"I can. Thirty tons every minute."

"More than seventeen thousand tons explosive yield every single day," Kimberly added. "That becomes tremendous energy, and—"

"Never mind that for the moment, Owen," Whiteson said, a bit more cross than he intended. Kimberly waited.

"You can stop the flow of energy at any time?"

"Yes, sir. You simply stop by not releasing the

pellets into the chamber or by interrupting the action of the laser beams."

"If your system was operating and the interruption, of *any* kind, was made, it would shut down?"

"Yes, sir."

Arthur Whiteson chewed his lower lips. "But that isn't what happened down in Cumberland, is it?" he said, and his voice was a whisper wearing a death mask.

"No, sir, it isn't."

"All right, Owen," Whiteson went on slowly, tiredly, "what happened? We're back to what you said before. One and one do not make two, I believe is how you put it."

"That's right. Anywhere else that might happen. But not when you reach certain levels of elemental forces such as we're dealing with. That's when you get this X factor, this unknown. We had it before in testing fusion bombs, and—"

"I'm familiar with that, Owen. Stay with this right now."

"We have a sun burning in our back yard, Mr. President."

Arthur Whiteson winced visibly. "A sun that's impossible."

"Yes, sir."

"But it's there."

"It is," Kimberly said, and he might have shouted it at the top of his voice.

"*Why* is it there? Why is the impossible suddenly real?"

"Mr. President, there are certain laws you can't avoid. Familiar laws, I will add. When we hit that D-T pellet with the laser beams, we create temperatures of a hundred million degrees. We've gone into that. The pellet must boil, of course, and it rips outward in all directions at a thousand miles a second. It doesn't go far because it's trapped by the magnetic force.

"It also does something else, Mr. President. You can't avoid Newton's law of action-reaction. We know that part of the hydrogen boils outward. But what remains must *implode*, that is, explode in reverse. In a moment of time that's much less than a trillionth of a second—how much less I have no idea—the density of that hydrogen pellet reaches incredible figures. Long ago we estimated the density to be thirty to fifty times greater than uranium."

Kimberly had a troubled look on his face, and his brow furrowed more with every passing second. "What's happened is that everybody was wrong about that density. We were scaling down according to classical laws. They don't apply in this sort of situation.

"We went far past the density that exists within the sun. We may have gone fifty, a hundred, a thousand times or even far more than that, in terms of mass greater than uranium. We simply *don't know*—"

"Tell me what you believe," the president said. His voice was calm, his demeanor soothing, but his mind whirled with what he was afraid to hear.

Kimberly took a deep breath. "On a microcosmic scale, Mr. President, I believe we have duplicated the energy release that takes place within the core of a collapsing star."

Arthur Whiteson felt as if he had been given a numbing mental blow.

"There is every danger, there's always been this

bloody danger," Kimberly was saying, "that we have created a space warp. That's what I meant when I said that one plus one do not equal two." He stumbled over his words for a moment. Was it one plus one does not equal two? Maybe—oh, to hell with it.

"A space warp," Arthur Whiteson echoed.

"Yes, sir."

"You're serious."

"Absolutely, Mr. President."

"Space warp, huh?"

"Yes, sir."

"It warps space." That should have sounded ridiculous, but it didn't.

"Yes, sir. It does."

"Uh, Owen, isn't it true that space and time, or perhaps you just call it space-time, are one and the same?"

"Yes, sir. They are."

"You're telling me, Professor, that what's burning in Cumberland is warping time?"

"I am, Mr. President."

"But that's ridiculous. It's impossible!"

"Yes, sir, it is."

Kimberly's calmness was maddening to Arthur Whiteson. "How the devil can you sit there like a statue making statements like that!"

"Because they're true."

"I hardly see how I can believe it."

"Then, Mr. President, and meaning no disrespect, *you* tell *me* what's burning in the Cumberland reservation. Because that also is absolutely, utterly impossible."

"Don't say it, Owen. It's impossible, but it's there."

"Yes, sir. And it's not going to go away."

8

President Arthur Whiteson felt himself swept along
a turbid river of disbelief. Warping time? It was—
well, it was insane. It violated everything he had
ever known, had learned, had had demonstrated
to—

Wait. What was it Albert Einstein had said so
long ago? Whiteson couldn't remember the exact
words, but he remembered enough. Einstein had
said that common sense consists of those layers of
prejudice established in the mind before the age
of eighteen. Perhaps it was sixteen—no matter.
The meaning was clear beyond dispute. He couldn't
rely on his common sense in this matter because it
lacked a foundation on which to rest. Yet it was—it
was mad!

Again he forced that thinking to a halt. He must
stay away from preconceived absolutes. Think; he
ordered himself. Go back a hundred or two hundred years. No, just a stinking century all by itself.
Just one century. Go back that far and try to prove

to those people with words alone that in this year of 1980 the program to reach the moon was past history. Tell them that nine great spaceships had orbited the moon, that twelve men had kicked up dust on that world so impossibly beyond the reach of the race of man. Explain, if he could, that we had peered into the bowels of Martian volcanos, that ships had settled on the thickly heated soup of the Venusian atmosphere, that we knew what Mercury looked like from a hundred views, that we had sniffed at the clouds of Jupiter and marvelled at our photographic reports from Saturn, and that we had sent a ship on its way out of the solar system toward another star. All that was fact, was past, and even now it seemed impossible.

How could he possibly explain a heavy mass of metal no larger than a grapefruit that in an instant could annihilate the greatest city on earth? Could he explain the diode, the transistor, the printed circuit, or even the computer? Dare he try to tell anyone that men who had lost limbs could now wear bionic replacements that were part and parcel of the body, that artificial eyes had been created, that we could transfer hearts from one human to another, that . . .

The president forced himself to take several long, deep breaths. He was unaware that the color had left his face. But he did know that he had made a decision, that he was moving *with* this strange man closeted in this room with him, that he must grasp belief. And yet, he needed to know more, to pound into his own skull what logic, common sense, and rationale all shouted at him to reject.

Because if he were wrong, the consequences would be fatal.

"Owen, you're not just tossing a favorite theory into my lap, are you?"

Gravely and ponderously Kimberly shook his head. "No, sir. I wish that was it, but it isn't."

"You'll have to break it down for me."

Kimberly's laugh was harsh, without humor. "I don't know if I can, Mr. President."

"You'll damned well try, Owen. If all the other things you've said are true, then you're forcing me to make decisions that, right or wrong, are going to affect the affairs of this country and much of the international community—the whole planet. So *try*—and in a way I can hang onto after you've left this room."

Kimberly's misery was evident. "I feel as if I'm in a position of trying to warn you about the end of the world," he said slowly. He shifted several times in his seat, his itch of acute discomfort running from his brain into his body.

Arthur Whiteson looked up. My God, it was morning. He blinked at the shaft of morning sunlight that penetrated the room like a phantom pillar. Birds sang in trees just outside the room. The distraction was overwhelming. He had visions of feathered creatures swooping down endless corridors of time. "Go ahead, Owen, if you would."

Kimberly shifted again in his chair. "The only thing I can tell you as a start, Mr. President, is don't fight it. I mean that, sir. It's the only way. Trying to understand, to really comprehend time and its twisting, or whatever, is simply beyond your means or mine. We're like natives in some distant land seeing a solar eclipse for the first time. We know it's absolutely impossible, it's terrifying, but it's there, and we have no choice but to believe. The evidence is darkening the sky, it's raining its shadows and gloom all about us, and no matter what we do, then, or later after it's gone, we cannot escape what happens. Even if we attempt to force it out of our minds, we know that somewhere in a corner of whatever consciousness there is that makes up the mind, it will hide and wait for us there, inescapable.

"Sir, in the last ten years we've destroyed almost every concept on which hard, practical astronomy was built. This past decade has made a mockery of the standards we used to judge this world and the universe. If you think that warping time—causing it to bend, twist, tear, rip, distort or whatever—is beyond reality, then you absolutely must understand that every single day we're given a real head-thumping with having to accept the existence of black holes."

"That's a star discovered only in recent years, isn't it, Owen?"

"Sir, it's the *absence* of a star. We don't know what a black hole is; we know what it was. We know how it comes about, and we know a little about what it does, but what we do know is a rape of everything else we know. If that sounds confusing to you, I—"

"Strangely enough, it makes sense. It's more like politics than you'll ever know," Whiteson smiled.

"Now you're losing me," Kimberly offered in mild rebuke.

Whiteson gestured him on.

"Imagine a star with several times the mass of our own sun," Kimberly said, suddenly serious. "The star explodes. It happens all the time. But if the star is that big, at least two to three times our solar mass, you get a supernova that's beyond conceiving. Imagine, if you will, sir, a single star putting out more energy in an instant than our whole galaxy of billions of stars burned in an entire year.

"Now, the star explodes, as I said, but at the same time, and this is simultaneous, it implodes. Until recently, Mr. President, we really weren't aware, in the meaningful sense, anyway, that what was happening was a gravity explosion. Pure, naked gravity run amuck. Not so long ago, we couldn't even think in those terms. I mean, we know about stars that burn out and become white dwarfs. That's a burned-out cinder of a star, and it's about the size of this planet. Try to picture that in your head. A star that has ninety-nine percent of all the mass in this solar system, squeezed down to the size of our world."

"You're squeezing my head in much the same way, I'm afraid," Whiteson said.

"Yes, sir," Kimberly said, seeming to ignore the mild complaint. "But the making of a white dwarf is a slow process that takes many billions of years. It's an orderly procedure, and at the end of it all, with a healthy enough explosion, we have a white dwarf. They're as common throughout the universe as pebbles on a beach.

"But when you have the bigger stars, and they're unstable and they explode, we get down to what we call stars that are pretty mean, or even vicious, in what they do. The stage beyond the white dwarf is what we call a neutron star. Look," Kimberly said suddenly, "I know this seems like I'm dragging it out, but I'm not."

There was a feeble smile from the president, nothing more. Kimberly took a long breath and plunged on.

"Think of the atom. Only one part in a hundred thousand is matter. The rest of the atom is emptiness. When certain stars collapse, when they implode, they squeeze together the electrons orbiting about every nucleus of every atom in that star. Matter becomes impossibly compressed. What happens is that the star is squeezed down to a diameter of only ten kilometers, and—"

"I knew I'd come to hate the metric system, Owen. My head hurts. You'd better tell me—"

"We started out with a sun twice the mass of our own, and after the explosion-implosion, it's mashed down to a star only six miles in diameter." Kimberly cracked a knuckle, unaware of the movement. "It still has the mass of our own sun, but it's only six miles in diameter! Did you ever use a sugar cube, sir? On a neutron star, it would weigh over a trillion tons! If such a thing were ever placed on the surface of the earth, faster than you could think of it, it would whip to the core of this planet. Our total destruction would take place in less than a second.

"You see, sir," and it was obvious Kimberly was struggling to keep all this clear for the president to comprehend, "the gravity pressures of a neutron star are so fantastic that the electrons have been squeezed down from their orbits and rammed into the protons of the nucleus. That changes everything in the star to neutrons, and the star is one single mass of neutrons squeezed together."

Kimberly reached into a pocket, withdrew a handkerchief, stretched it out taut, and then twisted it. "On the surface of a neutron star, gravity is so immense it twists space-time just like I'm twisting this cloth. I'm talking about gravity that's one hundred thousand million times greater than we're feeling right now. We've been to the moon, sir, and we needed twenty-four thousand miles an hour to get there. To escape from a neutron star, we would need a speed of two hundred and twenty million miles an hour. We can barely conceive of such velocity.

"But the point I really want to make is that on a neutron star the mass is so incredible that time slows down permanently. Time as we know it no longer exists. If you had a clock that could operate on the surface of a neutron star, it would run about ten percent slower than it runs on this world. Sir, that's a time bend, a curvature of time, and it's not theory."

Arthur Whiteson stared unblinking at him. "I don't know whether to consider you some sort of hero or to kill you," he said finally. "Bring it to a point, Owen. Make it fit with the problem we face. To hell with theory or not-theory. *Make it fit.*"

But Owen Kimberly was beyond being put off by any remarks from Arthur Whiteson or anyone else. Talking to this man had helped clear away the wisps of confusion in his own mind, for he was still staggered by the realization that the worst nightmare he had ever imagined, and indeed had warned other scientists about, had become real and was a horrendous dragon breathing down all their necks.

"Yes, sir, I'll do just that. I'm coming to the crux of all this."

"Thank the Lord for that," Whiteson murmured.

Kimberly ignored him. "The neutron star, Mr. President, is simply a transition on the way down to the black hole. In fact, compared to a black hole, the neutron star I've just described, with all that incredible mass and slowing down time, is as light and airy as cotton candy.

"The black hole is a gravity-time vortex. That's the best description I can give you. It's a whirlpool that twists and bends and does God knows what else to time. Nothing can ever escape its grasp. Please try to keep that in your mind. *Nothing*, including light, can ever escape a black hole. Where a black hole is concerned, there is no such thing as mass, time, size, or shape. We started out with a star several times the mass of our sun, and in an instant it's imploded down through a white dwarf, down through a neutron star and beyond, and—"

"You're telling me what it isn't. Tell me what it *is.*"

"We don't *know*. What I'm trying to make you understand, and you'll see where it all fits in just a moment, is that a black hole has established a gravity field that's infinite. We have a follow-the-leader situation. If you have infinite gravity, you have infinite acceleration, and if you've got infinite acceleration, you destroy time—and space along with it, since they can't be separated.

"Maybe it will have more meaning if I tell you that infinite acceleration means exceeding the velocity of light. Everything you've ever been told tells you this is impossible. It can't happen. Under every rule we know, it's impossible. Think about what I said. Infinite acceleration, infinite mass. Space and time share the same fabric of existence.

The black hole utterly destroys that fabric, so time is destroyed along with it.

"You see, when you have infinite acceleration, a trillionth of a second is quite the same as the lifetime of this entire universe, which we've measured to be fifteen or twenty billion years. I must return again to what I said before: there's no time, mass, size, or shape any more. The fact that there's *no size* is everything to the problem we face right now."

Kimberly paused for a breath. He wiped his face with the handkerchief he had twisted and pulled in his hands.

Whiteson had caught his drift. "All right, Owen. Tie the last pieces together. How does this affect what's happening in Cumberland?"

"I wish I could be more certain, but—"

"Goddammit don't hedge now!"

"I need more details," Kimberly said stubbornly. "But I think I've got a handle on the problem. It is my opinion, Mr. President, and I state this as a preliminary judgment, based on what we've heard from Drs. Clayton and Farrel, that the very existence of a sustaining fire of thermonuclear origin means we've created a gravitational field beyond anything we dreamed might happen. It's being contained by the magnetic field, the force field."

Whiteson's eyes widened. "Unless I've gone mad, I'm beginning to think you're telling me we have some sort of a black hole on our hands."

Kimberly's respect for the president was evident. "Yes, sir. On a scale vastly smaller than stellar, we may have just that. The fusion fire burning inside that bottle is patently impossible by every rule and law of science we know. So it's something with which we've never dealt before, and the *only* correlation is along the lines of a black hole. I've stressed again and again that size has no meaning where infinite acceleration is concerned. Within the finite field of that force field, the gravity field of the earth, that fire we ignited in Cumberland, in some way, somehow, has warped space-time about itself. However it has happened, it's managed to rupture whatever gravity-magnetic field exists between universes.

"And *that's* why the fire will not go out despite the fact it's not being sustained by anything we do. It doesn't need the D-T pellets any more. It doesn't need the laser beams. It is feeding on its own energy source from somewhere *beyond* this earth, through whatever manner it has twisted space-time.

"It no longer exists in this universe. Or it won't for very much longer."

Arthur Whiteson felt an incredible calm about him. He was through the thickets, back to the problem, finally able to think about a solution—if there was any . . .

"That's what you meant when you said it must grow."

"Yes, sir. If it hasn't gone out, it's going to feed, it *is* feeding, and it will feed on what's available."

"The mass of this world," Whiteson said.

"Yes, sir."

"What—then?"

"It will begin to expand its gravitational field in *our* space-time. It will draw in enormous mass—I don't know from where, but I'm afraid—"

"Yes, *yes?*"

"I'm afraid *we*—this planet—will be its beginning of growth." Kimberly looked up. Whiteson had no doubts that the enormity of what he had struggled to understand had hit Owen Kimberly with full force. "The mass will increase slowly at first, and then enormously. If this happens, then the fire—the focal point of this distortion—will begin to sink into the crust of the earth. As this happens, it will expand the immediate area of its effect. This can—well, it can happen in any one of several ways."

"But you believe implicitly that it will happen?"

"Yes, sir, I do. A warping effect on the immediate gravitational field, perhaps. Certainly an intense, almost a violent ionization of the atmosphere. Its effects will be progressive. Where the planetary crust is involved, it could melt it, crack it open, vaporize it—I simply cannot predict accurately at this point."

"Where does it stop?"

"It may *not* stop. On what we would call a microcosmic scale, it could become the equivalent of a black hole. It might even *be* a black hole." He hated himself for that much certainty in his answers.

Whiteson gestured impatiently. "If it increases its mass, what happens?"

Kimberly surprised him by answering with a shrug, as if he no longer wanted to commit himself to words.

"Beyond a certain point—could we still stop it?"

"No." Kimberly was emphatic in his reply.

"You mean unlimited growth?"

"Not growth. *Effect.*"

"You're talking about a point of no return."

"Yes, sir."

"What happens before that? What signs? What do we look for?"

"There'll be a bending of gravitational and electromagnetic fields. Radiation will pour out from the increasing mass—*not* size. It won't get any bigger in terms of volume or the space it occupies, but its effect will grow. The increase in radiation would take, oh, I don't know how long it will take, but the outpouring of radiation will sooner or later make a hash of the magnetic bottle they're using. It will hold for a while, though."

"How long?" The president pounced on the remark.

"I don't know for how long because I still don't know the characteristics of the fields involved. I just don't know."

"Owen, what will happen when the magnetic bottle, our force field, finally gives way?"

Kimberly laughed harshly, a skeletal rattle deep in his throat. Everything felt utterly unreal to him, this moment, what they discussed, what was happening in Cumberland.

"It means," he said slowly, "that the heat created the instant when a hydrogen bomb is exploded will be released into the atmosphere. But not for just a fraction of a second or for long seconds or even minutes. I'm talking about hours. I even hesitate to say for day after day because the earth itself might not last that long. You simply can't have that kind of temperature without turning the atmosphere itself into a furnace. You'd have winds of thousands of miles an hour. It would destroy everything on the earth's surface."

"If what you say is right," the president asked carefully, "can the magnetic bottle be strengthened to give us more time? To study the problem, to look for a solution?"

That, at least, Kimberly *did* know. "Yes," he said, and he thanked his own personal gods for that answer. He thought of the heat spreading across the surface of the earth, melting the air, concrete, steel, mountains, creating a constant hammering shock wave that never ended, that would finally melt bedrock and boil the oceans and—

He squeezed his eyes tightly shut to chase away the horrendous visions. They could hold back the *thing* inside that magnetic bottle for only so long and no longer.

Apparently the same thought had come to the president. He studied Owen Kimberly. "I must repeat myself. You are telling me, sir," he said quietly, "that this fire, or whatever it is, could destroy this entire planet?"

"Not could. Will. If it's not stopped, then it will consume this planet. It will build slowly and finally reach a catastrophic climax. We will go nova."

He hated the line that came to his lips. "And even Mars will get very warm."

9

"Owen, you seemed to make one point quite clear. Through your explanations, everything you said, I found you using the word 'if.' More specifically, you said catastrophic events were inevitable if the growth, or increase in mass, of this fire were not stopped."

Kimberly paused, grasping a moment to try to understand what the man meant.

"Dammit, you did say that, didn't you?" Whiteson demanded.

"Well, yes, sir, I did, but—"

"That means it *can* be stopped, doesn't it?"

"I *think* it can."

"But you're not questioning its effects if we don't try to stop it."

Kimberly shook his head in a sudden, almost violent motion. "No, sir, there's no question."

"Then you're going to try to put out that fire, Professor."

"Me?"

"Who the hell am I talking with? Do you see anyone else in here with us?"

"Uh, no, sir, but—"

"Don't go weak-kneed on me now, Owen. I need more information from you." Whiteson didn't like the slow but unmistakable slump in Kimberly's shoulders, the cloak of imminent defeat he had started to wear at the conclusion of hearing his own shattering words.

"How long do we have, Owen?"

"I, uh—"

"For God's sake—"

"One month. I hope. Maybe a month, and I can't get away from that maybe, and, as far as I can tell right now, sir, that's an outside figure."

"Tell me how you'll try."

Kimberly seemed to shake off the cloying fog that had collected about him. "One thing is certain. I had enough bad moments when I did government research to know that if I'm going to be able to do anything at all, then whatever I need, with whatever authority, must be settled before I leave this room."

Whiteson pondered the words, nodding slowly, more to himself than to Kimberly. He gave a sudden sharp look at the other man. "And if you don't receive that authority?"

Kimberly's smile was unexpectedly warm, as if he had disengaged himself from what was happening. "Then, Mr. President," he said softly, "I will return to St. Cloud to marry the woman I love and spend the final month of the human race with her and her children. It's as simple as that."

"I'm glad to hear that," said the president.

Kimberly was caught unaware. "What?"

"When a man reaches an impasse, Owen, and he has a choice for frustration to the last moment or has enough sense to know when he ought to be at peace and he selects that peace over all else—well"—Whiteson shrugged—"it tells me much about the man himself. You see, Owen, solving this crisis is going to take more, at least I feel this way, from human intuition, guts, whatever it is, than what we're going to get from straight technology. I have a man with me who's willing to take of the last drink from his cup of life. That gives me hope. You realize, of course, you're asking for what amounts to dictatorial powers, don't you?"

Again Owen Kimberly was startled by Arthur Whiteson's words. He started to repeat his "What?" of before, changed his mind abruptly, and shifted his thoughts along the same lines as the president's.

"I don't care what it's called. Or what it takes. Any discussion of limitations of money, manpower, or authority or whatever else is involved is asinine." He brought himself up short for the moment, examined the other man's impassive face, and went on.

"There's just no room for argument or contest. I'm not trying to sell you anything, Mr. President. If you recognize what is happening, what could happen—"

"Oh, I do, I do," Whiteson murmured.

"Then," Kimberly went on, "I must be supported in full, without question, and you, sir, simply must back up everything I need."

"Or demand," Whiteson offered.

"Yes, sir," Kimberly said firmly. "Or demand." He held his words as Whiteson rose to his feet and began to pace the room. "I might add, Mr. President, there'll be precious little time, or even none at all, to explain, to provide justification, or—"

Whiteson stopped pacing and held up a hand. "I've got the message, Owen. You'll get whatever you need." He turned away to resume his slow pace and kept talking without looking at Kimberly. "Where do you want to work?"

"Why, at the test site, of course. In Cumberland. The computer system there is the best, it's tied in to the fusion program, and I'll be able to work with Clayton and Farrel."

"Good." Again that inexplicable pause, the shifting of mental gears, the long unblinking look. "You realize, Owen, that if you fail in all this, you'll never be welcome again in the White House."

The remark was so ludicrous they grinned at one another. The naked smile in the teeth of annihilation.

"I want to know something else, Owen, especially now that you know you'll get everything you need. How much time do we have?"

Kimberly blinked his eyes. Hadn't they just gone over this same point? "Why, we talked about that, sir. A month. That's—"

"One month."

"Why, yes, sir."

"At least you haven't changed your estimate from a few minutes ago."

"But why would I do that?" Kimberly was getting confused.

"Because you would be very surprised at how men change their minds when they have moved from a position of having nothing to one of having everything they ask for. What's your next move, Owen?"

Kimberly took a deep breath. The impact of what was happening was just beginning to seep into his brain. He had been up so many hours now, had traveled so far, to be plunged into an abyss with the president of the nation, and now he had to face what lay ahead. Suddenly, he felt almost overpoweringly weary. It was not until this moment that he realized the incredible stamina of Arthur Whiteson, who every day had to face crises that, in many ways, had to be as appalling as this matter placed before him now.

And what must be even worse was that while Owen Kimberly flew south where he would challenge the fusion dragon, this man must remain here, in this building, to run the country, facing the same problems as before, wrestling with political chicanery and power thrusts of the Russians. And the worst of it all had to be that Arthur Whiteson would be *playing* the role of president just as much as living it, because his world would be little less than a mockery if Kimberly failed.

But, thought Kimberly, I will concentrate on what I have to do, and this man will support me to the fullest, all the while acting out his extraordinary game of blind man's bluff to the rest of the world. Yet, here he is, fully aware and fully supporting what I need and what we will all need. Then, the moment I leave here, he will turn to the rest of his antagonists, who are endless and as varied as the minds of men themselves. And none of them, or only a few of his closest confidants, will know that every day the last month of the world comes nearer.

He forced himself back to the moment, pushing away his sudden appreciation of this most extraordinary man who was the president. What had the president asked? Of course; what he had to do now.

"There are certain things to set in motion," Kimberly said, ticking off requirements. "I'll need quarters in Tennessee. Not just living quarters, but something right next to my office, the lab, where I can stay overnight if need be. I'll need a car. Above all, a staff with which I can work. I can select them when I get there. No. I can list several of them before I leave here and get them started to Cumberland. So that—we can do that?" He looked directly at the president as he voiced the question and received a quick nod in answer.

"One of the most important things is—" he hesitated—"a direct link from wherever I work, and wherever I sleep, to the main computer. I—well—I get strange ideas sometimes, in the middle of the night, I mean, and if I can have everything right there at my side, I can—"

Arthur Whiteson waved aside the growing verbal list. "Those are details, Owen. You can dictate them to a secretary after we're through, and it will all be started at once."

"Yes, sir. May I ask if living quarters are available right by the fusion center?"

"They are. It will be taken care of by the time you reach Cumberland." Whiteson waited.

"All right. Like you say, I'll do the rest with a secretary. But there's something else, Mr. President, that *you* must do, and you only."

Whiteson's brows rose in a silent question.

"You've got to talk directly with the Russian premier, Mr. President. No cables, no envoys, no messages. Forgive me if I sound as if I'm giving orders, but—"

"But you are," Whiteson reminded him. "Why are you so specific about my means of communication, however?"

"Because they've also been working on a fusion program, just as hard and for just as long as we have. However, they have taken several approaches to solving controlled fusion that differ from ours— tackling the problem in a different way, as it were. What's important is that they have brilliant men involved in their program, and there's every chance they may know some things in this area that we don't, just because of the avenues they're traveling. Anything could help. I want their best people working with me in Cumberland. And, please, sir," Kimberly tacked on to his explanation, "no problems with security."

Whiteson absorbed the request, thinking it over for several moments. "That's easier said than done."

"But why? How could security or anything else come into—"

"I didn't even mention security. Not from my viewpoint. You know and I know what's involved, Owen. They don't know, and they may not believe—"

"Then tell them. You're offering an open door to our entire program without asking a single thing in return! Surely even the Russians, their premier, can't fault that kind of open door."

"You haven't dealt with them, Owen. You—"

"But I *have*. Sir, while I'm here, right now, please get that call started. Talk with their premier. Tell him it's absolutely essential I talk right away with Vasily Tretyakov. He's one of the top men in their science academy, and he heads their fusion program. He'll understand. He'll see what we're facing. And once he gets here and sees that damned thing burning, well—"

Kimberly finished with a shrug. It was eloquent enough. My God, if he had to argue this point, there wasn't any use in even starting for Cumberland. He'd just go back to Colorado and to hell with it all.

He took a deep breath. "Tretyakov won't need any speeches, sir. He'll understand they've *got* to work with us or burn with us."

Whiteson chuckled. "Forgive my sense of the macabre. That's the only way we've stayed out of a war so far. You've got it, Owen. The call will be set up right away. Your list is growing. Keep it to the essentials."

"Yes, sir. There'll be certain people critical to my work. May I suggest that as soon as I prepare a list of names that you speak to each one personally? They'll have to hear from you about my role in Star Bright. The last thing we want or need is a contest in ego or personality about who's running the show, and there's no way we can avoid resentment at what people will consider heavy-handedness on my part. Anyone who's involved will have to be set straight at once."

"Done," Whiteson said. "What else?"

Kimberly rose. His joints were stiff; he hadn't realized how long he had been sitting. "A personal thing." He saw a sign of impatience on Whiteson's part.

"Go *on*," Whiteson prodded.

"My fiancée. I want her with me. We may not be successful. I'm sure you understand that. And the thought of our not being together—well, what I'm trying to say is—"

"I know what you're trying to say. I understand, and I concur. I suppose you want to get her and the children yourself?"

Kimberly's relief was immense. "Yes, sir, I would like to—"

The president broke in, almost rudely. "Out of the question, professor. All these rules and requirements you've been spouting to me apply just as well to you. You'll give the orders in this save-the-world show of yours, Owen, but you'll also *take* your orders from me. I sympathize with you. I understand Angela has also worked as your assistant?"

"Why, yes, but—"

"Good. We'll take care of things, Owen. But when you leave this room, you're going to prepare that list we've been talking about, and then you're getting on a jet straight from here to Cumberland."

"But my papers, my notes—"

"Everything in your home except your furniture is already being gathered for shipment to your quarters at Cumberland. The vice president has listened to this entire conversation, starting with my discussions with Pound, Clayton, and Farrel. He has already talked with Angela. She's helping gather your papers. She and the children will join you tomorrow, perhaps the day after, but no later than that. The situation, or as much as we could discuss on the phone, has been explained to her. She is cooperating fully. Is there anything else?"

Dumbfounded, again overwhelmed, Kimberly shook his head. Whiteson came to Kimberly's side and rested a hand on his shoulder.

"All right, then, Owen, it's time to go to work. I might add that I've also come to a personal decision these past few hours, and I'm going to indulge myself in those feelings. I have two sons and a daughter who are in different parts of the world. You're aware that their mother died some time ago."

Kimberly felt the other man squeeze his shoulder gently. "I'm bringing them home to be with me. To be here at my side in this month to come. As you say, it may be our last."

Book II

Book II

10

Fifty miles from Cumberland, Owen Kimberly saw the first vivid flashes of lightning. The small Rockwell jet trembled as they breached the first nudges of turbulence, and Owen Kimberly cinched his seatbelt tighter. The copilot looked back through the open cockpit door of the Sabreliner and waved reassuringly. Kimberly returned his gaze to the storm line they were approaching. The clouds were both white and black, and a purplish-yellow haze, a dirty scum in the sky, was spreading steadily. Some of the great cumulus clouds were caught by the jet streams of higher altitudes, their tops shorn clean as if cut by a vast and invisible scythe. More eye-catching to Kimberly were several parallel lines of stratus cloud, all running together at an angle to the great storm line. They looked like ribbon highways waiting for something to rush along their surface. Then they exploded silently, spreading apart, and shafts of sunlight dazzled earthward, cutting through the haze to the rich countryside.

They were descending steadily, the pilots turning the jet in order to stay clear of the thunderstorm cells. Kimberly was unaware that this airplane had been given the same air traffic control clearance as Air Force One and that every other plane in the air was being directed away from their line of flight. Their plane was constantly monitored by radar, and the pilots were never out of conversational control of men on the ground.

The plane skirted a muscled thunderhead, the air now alternating gold and gray as they slipped through sun and shadow. Closer now to Cumberland, Owen saw the earth as a running pattern of light tans and browns, patchwork quilts set against rolling dark green hills. At a distance, rounded mountains were suddenly visible, their green blanket burnished gold from the effects of haze and sun. They passed over a reservoir, man-created lake with no distinctive shape, but with branches thrusting out in all directions, poking into the wells of rapidly rising hills. There were ridges as well, jutting starkly like skeletal backbones from the land.

Kimberly was grateful for these moments as they descended steadily; he had come to ignore the sudden punching effect of turbulence, for he knew that once he accepted it, his body moved easily with the motions. Thus, he was free to have what he felt might be his last solitude for a long time to come. Or for too short a time. No matter at *this* moment; he was content to drink in the sights all about and below him, and to observe from this temporary vantage point the land where he might live out his last month on this world.

The plane made a wide turn, and now he was

looking into the sun, the roads winding along the surface transformed into glowing ribbons of reflected light. Railroad tracks that from the air so often blended into surface features came alive as long, sinuous, impossibly thin, and extended serpents winding away into the obscurity of the horizon haze. Rivers and streams leaped into prominence as flashing, twisting streamers of light given magical qualities by the sun.

A dark cloud swept by, and the exposed sun brought sudden pain to Kimberly's eyes, jolting him with the realization that what existed within the deep, buried guts of the sun also raged on the earth not very far from where they were. He searched the ground, and as they turned again, he saw the enormous complex.

A huge, rounded, intensely white structure rose more than three hundred feet into the sky, a Taj Mahal of the future, containing within its massive dome the intricate mass of neodymium-glass lasers where—

It hit him then. Inside that dome the fire was burning. Right there, contained within a magic sheath of electromagnetic force, which itself was encased in a vacuum chamber.

A tiny, impossible shriek of raw energy. *Star Bright.*

He forced his eyes to move on, to study the tunnels of the evaporation system. He recognized the experimental power station and the grid of power lines stretching away like spider strands of burnished gold in the sun, lofting themselves gently into the distance and cresting haze-covered hills. He knew enough of the basic layout to recognize the administrative buildings, the rows of well-built

private homes, and apartments and other structures. It was expansive, neat, and above all impressive. It represented over four billion dollars,
he thought, and it damned well *should* have been
impressive.

Then it all snapped out of view as the Sabreliner
descended and touched down on the runway, directly within the AEC reservation. Kimberly felt
the wheels thudding onto concrete and saw high
steel fences flash by.

Every muscle of his body felt tired. As the
engines wound down, the sound might have been
his own body releasing its last dregs of energy. He
needed sleep desperately, and he knew it was the
one commodity he dared not savor.

Time would now be his most dreaded enemy.

"Dr. Kimberly, you don't know how pleased I
am to see you here." Kathy Farrel was standing by
a station wagon, waiting for him.

Owen Kimberly didn't try to hide his happiness
at seeing her. "Dr. Farrel, the pleasure is mu-
tual," he told her, waiting for his one bag to be
taken from the airplane to the car.

"I'll drive," she said after his bag was put in the
trunk. "That way I can give you an immediate tour
of the main buildings and let you know the more
important areas."

They got into the car, and Kathy started to drive
off but stopped. "Oh—just one moment."

Reaching into a pocket, she handed him an
identification tag. He studied it for a moment,
seeing his own face looking back at him. The card
bore his right thumbprint, and he knew at a glance
it was magnetically coded.

"It's the highest priority," she explained. "No doors are closed with that badge."

He started to smile his thanks, then changed his mind. Of course; what else had he expected?

"Every security office, every person with whom you might be involved, has a copy of this badge, a brief dossier on you, and their orders for maximum cooperation. What we've tried to do is reduce to its absolute minimum anything that might interfere with your getting right to work."

That he did appreciate, and he told her so. "What about living quarters?"

"It's all arranged, doctor," she said. "I'll stay with you until you're ready to retire for the night. At that time you'll be assigned permanent drivers and round-the-clock security guards. They'll double as guides and will handle whatever your working or personal needs might be. Any time you—"

"Hold on," he said sharply, his senses alert. "I didn't request anything like that. I don't need—"

She broke in with a gesture. "I'm sorry, Dr. Kimberly. Orders."

"Who the devil from?" he snapped.

"The president."

He had no immediate answer for that. So he simply let it lay there. "What are your—plans?"

Unruffled, competent, she drove through streets that still had little meaning to him. Homes and service facilities, mainly. He'd pay attention when she would say so. He knew she wouldn't waste time or energy.

"As I said, a quick tour of the main facilities. Maps have been prepared for you so you'll understand the layout, but they're for your information only. The people who will work for you will take care of what you need in that area. Once you see the setup here, the problems of where to go or where to find anyone will be handled for you so that you can concentrate on your—" she faltered for a moment, and he knew all was not entirely calm and collected behind that attractive face— "well, on what you came here to do."

If he was going to be kingpin, he might as well get to it. "Why were you selected to meet me, doctor?" he queried her. "Anyone else could do what you're doing. I would have thought you'd be in programming right now." It was less than kind, but she didn't seem to mind.

"Dr. Clayton felt it best if I met you. That way I'll be able to answer whatever questions you have on what we've learned since we last saw you. Also, the programming is being handled competently by my assistants at this moment. My presence is not needed. This is my rest period, and I agree with Clayton about your having your exposure in this manner. There's no time for lackeys or anyone else far down the complement of personnel here to provide your introduction to Cumberland."

"You seem to have it all in hand."

He noticed they were cresting a hill. Moments later the main fusion complex came into sight. The last rays of the sun splashed from the huge dome he had seen from the air. Had he not known its great size, he would have judged it closer.

"What about Miss Dobson?" he said after his brief study of the buildings they approached.

"I understand she'll be flying in tomorrow," Kathy Farrel replied. "Your papers are with her. The moment she arrives she'll be brought to the house reserved for yourself, Miss Dobson, and the children. Your rooms have been prepared. We were told Miss Dobson works as your assistant, so we have arranged for the children always to be with someone." She flashed him a smile. "I thought you would also be pleased to know that your dog will be with them."

His surprise and his pleasure were genuine. "Thor? That is good news." He felt suddenly warm toward this woman. "Thank you for all the detail. It will make things much easier."

"I sincerely hope so," she offered, and again he was seeing through the cloak of efficiency.

"How bad is it?" he asked. He had put off the question with necessary banality long enough.

She bit her lip, as much in pain, he decided, as in thought. "It's not good," she sighed finally.

"I'll need more than that, doctor."

"Oh, I understand. I'm just trying to replace my feelings with numbers that have meaning," she added quickly, "and that isn't as easy as it sounds. There's so much unknown here."

Kimberly nodded. "In its most concise form, then. I assume there's no loss in energy?"

"No, sir, there isn't," she said with a resignation he disliked at once.

"What about increase?"

"I wish I could say we knew for certain."

He found that incredible. "You mean you don't *know*?"

She shook her head quickly, almost angrily. "We don't *know* because we're dealing with unknowns, Dr. Kimberly. The evaporation system was designed for maximum sustained output, and it's working properly so we're managing to absorb the thermal release. We can't get radiation readings directly from the bottle because of the energy shield. Dr. Clayton and his team have been working day and night to produce some system that would provide meaningful readings, but—" Abruptly she stopped.

"But what?" he demanded. "This is energy we're talking about. Thermal, the entire band of radiative —well, surely you can tell if you're getting an increase?"

Again that stubborn shake of her head. "No, we can't. I wish we could, but there's something else. We don't know what it is. There's an X factor here, Dr. Kimberly, and—"

For the moment he blocked out her words. An X factor. The same thing he had said many years before and what he had said only hours ago to the president, He forced himself back to this moment.

"Manifestation?"

"Something is affecting the instrument readings. We're not certain what it is. But what we're indicating simply doesn't correlate with what we expected." She glanced at him. "You're the man we hope can tell us."

"At the first opportunity, Dr. Farrel, I want pendulums, of the highest sensitivity possible, placed in progressive positions outward from the energy source. I want continuous readings, all of them graphed, and a real-time computer readout of changes, flow, intensity—you know the rest. I want you to order those the moment you get to a telephone." He glanced around the station wagon. "That radio equipment. Can you use that as a telephone? If you can, I don't want you to waste any time."

"Yes, sir."

She rolled to a stop in a parking area and an armed guard came over to the car, checked their ID badges, saluted, then moved away. Kimberly didn't comment. There was no need to. This was parking privilege enforced with a vengeance, he thought. An excellent idea. Haggling over parking spaces or being forced to waste valuable time looking for one would be asinine. Then he remembered he wouldn't have that problem. He'd be driven to and from anywhere he wanted or needed to go. Kathy Farrel, ignoring him for the moment, was switched by radiophone to her office and spent several minutes giving specific orders to someone who worked for her. Kimberly listened; the pendulums would be installed within hours.

"Do you want the full tour now? Of the main facility?" she inquired.

That had been his plan, but he changed his mind. "No. I need to get into the fusion control room. I want to see the fire." He paused. "I want to see it right away."

It was more than mere impulse. There had been so little rest, so much numbing shock, that he knew he had insulated his mind against the macabre nature of what they faced. He needed to be jolted back to the present. And if nothing else, Kimberly judged of himself, he must *feel*, he must have that gut sensation of knowing what this was in terms of seeing the fire dragon. He knew he couldn't see it directly. Who wanted to be struck blind in an instant? But there would be a series of dark mirrors that progressively dimmed the nightmare of light.

* * *

They walked through long corridors, their heels echoing along hard floors. Some of the people they passed nodded to Kathy Farrel or stared with open curiosity at Owen Kimberly. He paid it all scant attention.

The interior of the center was a strange combination of monkish austerity with plush scientific and technological trappings. As they walked, Owen felt as if he were walking through a fusion temple. The security force here consisted of armed guards—military guards. They carried both sidearms and automatic weapons held at the ready, and there was a brisk and businesslike manner to their checking of credentials. As they neared the main control room, security became uncompromisingly strict. Their ID cards were presented to electronic scanners, and they each had to place their right thumbs against a scanning plate that fed directly to the security computer.

"This is to prevent unexpected or unauthorized changes in high-security penetration," Farrel explained. "The computer is kept on a real-time update of all changes in ID and is fed a list of those people authorized to go beyond these points."

"It seems to be overdone," he said, bristling. His old antagonists were all about him again.

"Last week you would have been right," she replied, untouched by his sharpness. "This week you're wrong, doctor. Word has been getting out that something terribly wrong is happening here. It's impossible to keep it a secret, I suppose. But an ugly mood is developing in the immediate countryside. We can hardly afford to ignore it. People are mounting a holy crusade against the atom as an instrument of evil."

He yielded, albeit grudgingly. He'd known of such reactions before when fission reactors went into operation. He was also aware that an angry mob, in which reasoning was snapped away from existence by emotion, could be a powerful, destructive force. If that became their problem, and it was, as Kathy Farrel said, a holy crusade, they'd be defending this place with awesome military power. Killing power. How strange, he mused. We will have to kill those people out there in order to protect other people. Jesus. He pushed it out of his thoughts. Someone else had that responsibility.

Then they were in the main control room. His earlier feelings of being in a temple were reinforced. To begin with, it was enormous. The high-vaulted dome reminded him of one he had seen in the great cathedral in Seville, Spain.

They went to the observation console. A series of mirrors and filters all led to a single study window. "We use about seventy reflectors, each with dimmers, before the light reaches here," Kathy explained.

He sat down in front of the console and glanced from the window to her. "Otherwise it's direct? I mean, not through a TV scanner?"

"That's right," she confirmed. "At the same time, we'll use an additional manual filter by this window for your first look. Then, when your eyes are accustomed to what you're seeing, you can reduce the filtering a bit. I assume," she smiled, "you want the maximum optical effect short of damage."

He did something she didn't expect. To hell with the filtering. He wanted, he needed, that impact. He saw the control buttons that opened the window to viewing and depressed the master button.

"Doctor Kimberly!" she cried out, but she was too late to stop him.

His own sound was a gasp, a shout of fright. Despite the system of reflectors and dimmers, it was painful to stare into the radiance streaming from the tiny star. The light stabbed with dagger points into his eyes, yet he knew he wasn't seeing the pinpoint of fusion flame. It was too small to be seen by the naked eye. It was so small that it couldn't have been seen without the aid of a microscope if it didn't have its savage glare. He saw only an effect, dimmed and filtered again and again and again, and yet it was so savage, so overwhelming, that it mocked the very meaning of the word light.

He sat back in the chair, silent, shaken to his core, and he closed his eyes. The after image of what he had seen danced and whirled along his optic system. He knew he'd see that ghostly effect for hours, perhaps for days. Good, he told himself. He had a headache he knew would stay with him. He had wanted the impact, by God, now he had it. Finally he opened his eyes and looked across the console at Kathy Farrel. Her expression was a mask.

"What does one say," he asked slowly, "when one looks at the fire of Creation?"

Her smile was forced, almost pained. "I would ask you to stop Creation."

He pushed back on his chair. "Yes, of course. One Creation in the life of man is enough, isn't it?"

He was shocked with his first look at Dr. Richard Clayton. The effects of fatigue and worry over their problem had heightened the cameo effect he had seen before in the man's face. Could he have lost still more weight? He seemed almost to levitate as he stood, swaying slightly, before Kimberly. If the lights behind the man had been bright enough, Kimberly felt that Clayton would have assumed an almost translucent effect.

Clayton's relief on seeing Dr. Owen Kimberly, *here*, was clear and unmistakable. Whatever human foibles that Clayton possessed, in terms of ego or authority or claim to ultimate intellect, had vanished. This was a troubled and a frightened man who understood very well indeed that their cooperation was everything.

They drank coffee in Clayton's office, and their preliminary conversation lasted only moments. Kimberly toyed with his cup. "Kathy told me you were experiencing an unexpected field," he said finally.

Clayton nodded. "Unexpected is right." He brushed hair from his forehead in a nervous gesture Kimberly would come to know well. "Obviously when she described it, you had some understanding, or, at the least, you weren't too surprised."

Kimberly nodded his assent. "I'm in the same boat as the rest of you," he offered. "Except that I've spent more time looking at possible effects no one else seemed to consider. That's not a criticism, Dr. Clayton. I—"

"No offense, no offense," Clayton told him at once. "We're all beyond that. My God, Kimberly, if putting me on the whipping post would help, I'd tie myself to the damned thing."

Kimberly was surprised, almost amazed. Pretentiousness had been this man's trademark, and now it was gone. It had been frightened right out of him. Very, very good; Clayton was a brilliant man, and if he threw all his mental weight into this, it could tip the balance.

"Let me try something," Clayton went on. "You've ordered pendulums placed in certain areas. That speaks for itself. Am I right in assuming you're looking for a magnetic effect that would decrease their movement?"

"Magnetic? That's one possibility," Kimberly answered. He pursed his lips. "But you may have hit on something. Kathy, would you please add to that request? I want additional pendulums, placed in order with the others, but I want equipment that's nonmagnetic. Even wood will do."

Clayton nodded to her. "Do it now," he directed, and she left the room.

Clayton turned back to Kimberly. "You're looking for a mass distortion effect, aren't you." It was a statement, not a question.

Kimberly nodded. "Perhaps. Like we've all said, there's an X factor. We don't know the increase in mass with which we're dealing. If it increases, if it begins to square itself, we could have a center of mass within the earth's gravitational field, and—"

"But enough for *distortion?*" Clayton obviously was rejecting the idea.

Kimberly shrugged at the interruption. "I suggest you rid yourself of any preconceptions, doctor. You'll only have to break them down as we go along."

"It's still—"

"Impossible?" Kimberly smiled. "So is our little bonfire. Now. I have a list of questions. Do you have the time to spend with me?"

Clayton both recognized and appreciated the

courtesy of Kimberly's question. They spent an
hour going back and forth on technical points,
sweeping from the mundane to the philosophically
outrageous. When they had finished, Kimberly
knew enough to recognize his worst fears, and
Clayton would be able to carry out his studies with
greater efficiency than before. Kimberly wanted
desperately to rest, but there was still one more
chore to do. He had to meet with the old man of
the program, Dr. Lawrence Pound. Pound may
not have been involved in the direct role of science, but he was still the top dog in administration
and control, and if Kimberly could obtain his willing cooperation—he wouldn't need enthusiasm and
didn't hope for it—Pound could keep the corridors
clear for work by them all without bureaucratic
friction.

Dr. Lawrence Pound was unruffled as he sat in
the comfort of an old armchair, his pipe held in
one hand, poised in a thin smoke cloud of its own
making. Dr. Lawrence Pound radiated—well,
Kimberly damned well didn't know what it was,
but after observing him, he began to understand.
In a swirling storm of human doubts and fears, the
old man was unruffled and untroubled; it was as if
he were in the eye of a hurricane, serene in the
midst of surrounding violence.

"I am glad, very glad indeed," Pound said with
an easy gesture with his pipe, "to hear what you
are saying." He smiled with yellow-stained teeth
at Kimberly. "I have been trying my best, of course,
to do everything requested by the president. In
his own words, or as close to them as I can remember, Professor, he directed me to function in

the manner of a snowplow. Yes, that was it, I'm
sure. You understand what I mean? My role is
that of a plow, a cowcatcher on our train of research." Pound chuckled with his own words. "Irregular, of course. Highly irregular, I might add."

Kimberly expected him to harrumph and wasn't
disappointed when Pound coughed and wheezed
as a matter of conversation. "But that is of little
consequence, Professor. Those are my orders. To
make certain nothing interferes with your work, to
accept that you are the absolute master of this
project, to—"

Kimberly broke in hurriedly. "I'd hardly call it
that," he protested.

"Tut, tut, my dear man! If the president of the
United States says you are the absolute master,
and those are his words, not mine, I have no objections. He should know, Professor, and I am quite
certain he does know. My job is administrative,
and I am simply answering the dictates of the
commander in chief."

Owen Kimberly was amazed. He had known
Pound years back, and he could be an irascible old
son of a bitch when someone interfered with his
neat, orderly world. Now it was turned upside
down, and the old man was as smooth as silk.
Kimberly didn't doubt that President Whiteson
had sugar-coated the pills he'd slipped the old
geezer, but who cared?

Pound had a twinkle in his eye. "Among other
things, Professor Kimberly, I'm also responsible
for your well-being. Might I say that the first
order of business for you, sir, is to get a good
night's sleep? You're showing the strain. Oh, I
know what's been going on, that you've had pre-

cious little time for rest, but you won't be worth a fig, you know, if you can't think straight. And nothing will help like sleep. Do you take warm milk before you retire?" Kimberly shook his head. "Ah, well, it wouldn't hurt, you know. Been doing it myself all my life, and I sleep as sound as a dollar." He chuckled. "Not that a dollar's worth that much, of course, not nowadays."

Kimberly let the old man ramble on. There was more to this than just Pound's acceptance of presidential orders. He was too calm. How could he ignore the burning in the control room?

He had to put the question to Lawrence Pound, to see what lay behind this serenity. And the answer he received dismissed the other questions in his mind.

"Why am I not upset like Richard or Kathy? Or yourself? Or even President Whiteson?" Pound laughed. "Because, my dear fellow, I simply do not believe all this nonsense about the end of the world. Oh, don't deny it, Professor Kimberly. It's the worst-kept secret of all. But do you really expect people like myself to believe the destruction of this entire planet and all the people on it is really so imminent?

"My dear, dear Kimberly, I have lived through too much, I have lived through too many wars, I've heard the thunder of the hooves of the Four Horsemen again and again. And if I've learned anything in this life, sir, it is simply that the dreaded apocalypse is more in the minds of men than in reality!"

To emphasize his words, Pound stabbed the air with his pipe, and a trail of ashes followed his sweeping movements. "I am a deeply religious man, Professor, and that has been a help in the midst of creating and watching hydrogen bombs exploding all over the place. That is why I took with such fervor to Star Bright. To think we can duplicate the energy in the sun for the good of man! That is our purpose here, to be in harmony with nature, to understand the secrets God has placed all around us, whether it be the beauty of the rose or the furnace within our sun. It is all one and the same, and this is simply one more test of us by the Lord, and I, Professor Kimberly, have more faith in the Supreme Being than to believe he could so utterly, so callously, waste the garden of wonder he placed here on this world. We are being tested, sir, and we—you and I and the others—are heeding the time of our tribulation. It is *good*, Kimberly, it is good, indeed. We are testing our mettle, we are improving the steel of our beings, and we are—"

A rifle shot cracked loud, and the window just behind Dr. Lawrence Pound's shoulder shattered, spraying him with flying glass. He wasn't hurt, but the lesson was implicit.

The old man was right. Star Bright—what was happening inside that huge dome—was hardly a secret any more. And there were fanatics out there who believed with all the religious fervor and intensity of Dr. Lawrence Pound, that Star Bright was the work of the devil, and its creators should be destroyed, or God would destroy one and all.

The first attempt to kill Dr. Lawrence Pound had almost succeeded. There would be more, Kimberly knew. They would all become targets.

11

He came awake slowly, fighting losing the warmth
and comfort of sleep, the total yielding of body
and mind to—

Angela shook him again, and he remembered
now. He had been here in Cumberland for two
days. It had taken that long for Angela to gather all
his papers and notes and to be flown in with the
children and his dog. Two days and nights. He
had slept only that first night, after the rifle bullet
had smashed the window and slammed into the
wall of Pound's office. He'd taken Valium then,
both to ease his tightening muscles and to bring
him down from the high-strung condition into which
he'd been pushed. The next day and night, he,
Richard Clayton, Kathy Farrel, and a dozen scientists went until dawn fighting theory and fact and
trying to find the unknown factor that haunted
them. They learned every day, they learned every
hour, and most of the things they learned turned
out to be ghosts that had to be hurled aside so

they might learn the true nature of the fire always burning nearby.

Then he had returned to the house assigned to him by the government and was astonished at the sight of barbed wire hastily thrown up around the place, steel shutters on all the windows, and armed guards everywhere. He thought then of the barricades at the beginning of the street. He hadn't had time to pay attention to what had been happening outside the laboratory, but here he was back at the same place where he'd slept, and there were all those cars, guards, and protective devices that hadn't been there when he had left in the morning. He went inside where a great furry creature hurled itself at him with tail-wagging joy, and he looked beyond the animal and saw Angela and the children smiling at him.

For the first time in days, he pushed the fire, if not from his mind altogether, at least from his direct thinking. The children were genuinely fond of Kimberly, and he made absolutely certain not to let Susan and Peter know the horrors lurking around tomorrow's dawn and every day after that. Angela had already started a pot roast, and Kimberly played with the children and the huge dog. He savored every moment, and although the children failed to see beyond the thinly veiled eyes that withheld what lay within, Angela knew. She loved and accepted his moment with this family. There would be time later.

So it came in darkness, when the house was quiet, the steel shutters closed, the guards outside by the barbed wire settled, the dog lying in the hallway between the two bedrooms. He sat in an armchair in her room with the lights dimmed, and they talked quietly, accepting this oasis, no matter how temporary, of protected quiet.

"It's crazy, you know," he said. "I've wanted so much to marry you and here we are together, locked in, really, and now the world's upside down and there's been no time for it. I—"

"We're not children, Owen. We can always have the ceremony. But from this moment on I want you."

"So do I, of course. But dammit, I want us *married*."

"Marriage is a state of mind."

"I know, I know, but—it's just something inside me, Angie. I've always thought of the marriage ceremony as a celebration of love. We can't do much with this insanity about us." He lifted an arm, letting it drop wearily.

She studied him carefully. "Oh, my dear, it really does mean that much to you."

He nodded. "It does."

"Do you believe in God, Owen?"

He was almost startled. "That's a strange question, here and now." He returned her smile. "Yes, I do."

"Then I am sure He permits special compensation. One does not need a temple priest at certain times. Come with me, my love." She went into the hall, the great dog instantly alert. "Stay," she commanded, with a hand signal as well as her voice. She pointed to the children's room. "Guard." The dog looked unblinking at them, and they knew he would not move.

She led Owen downstairs to the living room. He stood and watched as she lit three candles and arranged them, two atop the fireplace mantel, and one inside the fireplace. She turned off all the other lights in the room. She reached behind her neck and unclasped a gold chain from which a cross hung. Then she hung the chain along the edge of the fireplace mantel, so that when they came together before the fireplace the cross seemed suspended against a flickering glow in darkness. She took his hand and lowered herself to a kneeling position, motioning him to do the same. For a long moment they looked into the eyes of one another, holding hands. Angela then turned her body, still on her knees, facing the cross. Owen did the same and now his left hand held her right.

"Before God," she said in a hushed voice, "I love this man and cherish him, and so long as we may live, I wish him to be my husband, and ask for Your blessings."

He found himself unable to talk, and finally forced himself from a feeling of awe for this woman. In a single moment he had seen deeply into more of her soul than he had known before.

"Before God I love this woman, cherish her and adore her, and so long as time is granted to us, I wish us to be man and wife."

They stared at the cross and the flame, silent, until she turned to face him. "It is done, my husband." She saw tears on his cheeks.

"Now and forever," he said, his voice husky, and they carried the two candles from the mantel back to their bedroom.

"We'll tell the children in the morning," she said, and brought her body to his.

In the morning he fought awakening, but Angela was insistent, and when he detected the uncertainty, the fear in her voice, he was instantly alert.

"Owen—that sound. I'm not sure what it is, but it frightens me."

He went to the window, then remembered it was shuttered. But with the glass raised, they heard the distant sounds a bit more clearly. He heard what had disturbed her—light, popping sounds, stuttering.

Machine guns! They're shooting at something, he thought. Or someone. What the hell is going on?

He couldn't tolerate a lie, especially not between them. Returning to the bed he sat alongside her. "Trouble out there, Angie. Those are machine guns."

She nodded slowly. "It's come to that, then."

"You seem to know more than I do."

She sighed as she sat covered by the sheets, her knees tucked just below her chin. "You've been busy, love. I've had the chance to talk with the guards at the airport, the people who drove us here, the guards outside. They're grim, Owen. They talk. From what they said—and from the looks of this house itself—it sounds very much like we may be in for a siege."

He showed his surprise. "I had no idea it was that well known."

"It isn't, really. No one seems to *know* what's happening, but they're aware something is terribly wrong in here. Also, the security has been bungled. I mean, the army, I guess it's them, Owen, moved in with enough noise to wake the dead, and they're taking over everything in the countryside."

He nodded. "I suppose it could have been handled better. But that's easy enough for us to say. Did you hear anything that might pinpoint what's happening here?"

She smiled, shaking her head. "*I* know."

"You? How on earth—"

"I have read your notes, Owen, and talked with you, and—well, I know."

He stroked her shoulder. "You seem less frightened than the rest of us."

"Shouldn't I be? I've lived with death, and with life, and a long time ago I learned not to fear what might happen tomorrow. Especially, Owen"—and she reached for his hand—"when the only thing I can do is to help you. Fear won't contribute a thing, and I don't want to infect Susan and Peter. They know something's wrong, of course, but it's not immediate or personal or dangerous to them."

"Thank the Lord for that," he said quietly. "What about what you've heard?"

"Crazy things. Everything from a crashed spaceship to a hydrogen bomb that's on the edge of exploding and we don't have much of a chance to stop it."

He chuckled. "I wish it were a spaceship. Then we could hand the problem over to the people from 'out there' and let them handle it. But that other one you said—about the hydrogen bomb. It's amazing how people can state the ridiculous and yet be so close to the truth."

He shook his head. "I'll find out later just what's happening. It won't affect us here. Not," he added grimly, "after what happened with Larry Pound. That one shot may have been the best thing that happened. The security was increased, no one was killed, and even though the old man was given a glass shower, he wasn't hurt. In fact, it made him something of a hero to the staff. You know, stiff upper lip and all that."

She squeezed his hand. "Owen, don't discount the reaction beyond the fences to this place. I can sense something terrible happening."

He had learned never to discount her intuitive grasp of a situation. "That bad?"

"I'm afraid so. I don't *know*, of course, but—" She shrugged.

"We'll see, honey." He glanced at the clock on the end table. "It is time, my dear, to go slay dragons."

By that same afternoon he came to understand just how right Angela's feelings were. On the way to the laboratory with Angela, he noticed that their driver was armed, that they were preceded by a jeep with a .50 caliber machine gun at the ready, and followed by another similarly armed vehicle. Street barricades and armed men were everywhere, and helicopters overhead moved through slow patterns of search.

Kimberly felt annoyed with such an overwhelming presence of military strength and knew that until he found out just what was happening, and why the security was so intense, he would be distracted. After he reached the lab, he called Sam Bruno at the security office and told him to come right over. He arrived within a few minutes.

Sam Bruno was a heavyset bull of a man, and he rolled a cigar from one side of his mouth to the other. An ex-marine, judged Kimberly.

"You want it straight, Professor Kimberly?" without any preamble.

"There's no other way, Mr. Bruno. Straight and quick. No speeches please."

"Yes, sir. The shit's hit the fan. It's that simple. We had someone working deep inside this project, and he's scared witless, and so he ran straight to a local TV station and laid the nightmare stories right on their desk. They didn't know how true it was, they didn't even understand the bastard, but Star Bright is good copy, and anything that smacks of trouble or danger is juicy copy. The rest is chain reaction; the network picked it up, the wires ran with the story, and the scaremongers have been having a field day."

"But you said the man from here didn't really understand what was happening," Owen Kimberly protested.

"Yes, sir, but you've got to understand it couldn't have mattered less. There are smart people in the news business, and they began putting two and two together. Especially this Benedict fellow who's covering the White House. He has his contacts. He knows about your meeting the president, he got the times Clayton and the Farrel woman and Dr. Pound were there, and he just fit all the pieces together and wrote one hell of a story."

"Which claims?"

"He doesn't claim anything. He flat says something's gone wrong, run amuck, here in Cumberland. Christ, Professor, if he had made a claim, any kind of claim, our people could have denied it or answered it. But he didn't know for sure, and he said so. And that was the worst way to go at it because everybody out there who has a mouth or can get someone else to listen to him is shooting off his yap."

"That's talk and talk only."

Sam Bruno pulled the cigar from between clenched teeth and stared at Owen Kimberly. "The word's out that you're a straight guy, professor."

"I suppose that deserves thanks."

"You feel it does?"

"In your own idiom, Mr. Bruno, I don't much give a damn what the word is, either in the center or outside. Get to the point."

Bruno grinned at him. "The boys were right. You're straight Indian."

"Damn you, Bruno, lay it out or—"

"Sorry. You ever hear of a man called El-Asid? He's the leader of a wild new cult. He came out of nowhere, and he's got an incredible following already."

"El-Asid? No. Never heard of him."

"He's a fanatic, a lunatic. One of those shining-eyed freaks with a magnetic aura about him that people just can't resist. He absolutely mesmerizes them. El-Asid, by the way, isn't his real name, but that doesn't matter. What counts is that he's spreading the gospel that the people here in Cumberland are murdering the planet Earth."

"That *is* a neat turn of a phrase, Mr. Bruno."

"Sure, sure, but the thing is that people are starting to believe this nut."

"You mean because of what he's saying?"

"What else?"

"He's dangerously close to being right."

The cigar fell from Bruno's mouth. He stooped to pick it up, stared at it, then replaced it between his teeth. "Sorry."

"You recover quickly."

"You telling me the prophets of doom are right, Professor?"

"They could be. We're trying to find out right now."

"But it's possible?"

Kimberly took a long breath and leaned back in his chair. "To my everlasting sadness, it is."

"Oh, shit."

"Is that all?"

"No, sir, it sure isn't," Bruno said. He made an angry gesture. "This El-Asid is calling for a holy crusade against the Cumberland reservation."

"You seem to have it well in hand. I mean, with all the firepower I've seen around here."

"We've got a lot of State and National Guard troops, yes. But I don't know how they'll hold up against a mob gone ape."

"Explain that, please."

"Professor, this El-Asid is calling for a mass charge against Cumberland. He wants tens, maybe hundreds, of thousands of people to throw themselves into what he calls the cauldron of evil. They're to sacrifice their lives, anything, to tear this place apart."

"You said you had the National Guard here, didn't you?"

"Yes, but they're not seasoned, Professor. They're liable to come unglued when they have to start killing by the carload."

"You think it will come to that?"

Bruno forgot Kimberly's title or anything else. "Man, you don't understand! There are thirty dead already and maybe two hundred wounded or hurt, and they're just warming up. It's not their getting all the way in here, I'm worried about. They can do a lot of damage long before they reach this center. Power lines, things like that, and—"

"What about Dr. Pound? He's top man here. Have you taken this to him?"

"That old coot? Meaning no disrespect, Professor, but if we let Pound have his own way, he'd be on the main road opening the gates to those loonies and greeting them with flowers."

Kimberly remembered his conversation with Dr. Lawrence Pound and realized suddenly just how dangerous Pound had become. If he believed this was all some sort of neat little test from Upstairs, then he'd understand nothing about the urgent need for full security. And if they had any hope of success in their endeavors, the last thing they could endure was a screaming, killing mob raging through the place.

"Sam, you have a direct line to the White House?"

"The where? I've got connections, Professor, but nothing like *that*. I—"

Kimberly motioned for him to cut it short. He buzzed for the secretary assigned him. "Miss Bronson, get a call to the White House at once. Use the priority code assigned to me. I want to speak directly with the president, no matter where he is or who he is seeing. Put it through immediately."

Sam Bruno stared in disbelief at him, and Kimberly elected to wait out the expected call in silence. It came within three minutes, and he told the president, clearly and without embellishment, what was happening, what could happen, and that they needed absolute military cordoning off of the entire area. He put down the phone and turned back to Sam Bruno.

"Take your orders from no one but me," Kimberly said, "or anyone else I tell you. Are you tough enough for this job, Bruno?"

"Yes, sir."

"Then you handle this thing all the way, Bruno. Don't bother me with the details. But keeping a mob out just does happen to be a matter of life or death. If these facilities are damaged—well, there's a saying that you might just as well give your soul to God because your ass is going down the tube with the rest of us."

Bruno rose to his feet. "Yes, sir. Now let me ask you just one question, and then I can do what you want."

"What we *need*," Kimberly broke in.

"It all comes out the same in the end, sir. Would you mind answering one question for me?"

"Go ahead."

"I've got to issue a shoot-to-kill order for anyone who tries to break through the fence lines or the roadblocks."

"Do it."

"That includes men, women and kids—of any age. That means little girls, because people like these, who really believe that what they're doing is the only way to go, always bring their kids with them. If you were on a roadblock, Professor, and a bunch of little kids were coming at you, would *you* pull the trigger?"

Kimberly felt the color draining from him. "I—what I mean is—Jesus Christ, Sam I don't know."

"Not good enough."

"But why do I have to answer that? I won't be at the roadblocks, and—"

"Yes, you will. Maybe not in person. I want to be sure you understand what the hell this is all about, Professor. It's not some research project. If you give me the order to shoot to kill, then I want you to understand that every time a trigger is squeezed and people die, your finger is also on that trigger. And if *you* don't believe in all this— well, Jesus Christ, sir—how the hell do I tell my men to murder people?"

Kimberly felt his hands trembling. He thought of the fire, and he nodded slowly. "I understand, Sam. If I were there, I'd pull the trigger. I'd *have* to."

"Okay, then. That's the way we go." Sam Bruno started to leave, then turned back for a last word. "You pray much, Professor?"

"Lately, a lot more than usual."

"Gotcha, Professor. Next time you're at it try to put in a good word for me, will you?"

El-Asid may or may not have been a true believer on his own, but his followers were. Two hours after Sam Bruno left Kimberly's office, their assault began in earnest. A truck loaded with gasoline drums was driven at top speed through a roadblock, scattering stunned soldiers who fired off a few ineffective rounds. Sam Bruno was right. The truck was also filled with small children who were very clearly and plainly in sight, even though the vehicle was a bomb rolling at seventy miles an hour. It was rolling straight for a main generator building, only minutes after the orders had come through officially to stop anyone or anything making for the inner perimeter of the AEC reservation.

A tank blocked the road and fired a warning

shot that sent jagged metal screaming around the truck. It never slowed down. It was only two hundred yards away when the second round of ammunition hit the truck directly and turned it into an instant inferno filled with writhing bodies. Then the truck exploded, and pieces of metal and bloody chunks of children rained down on the shocked soldiers. The sounds of vomiting were heard over the crackling roar of flames.

It had begun.

12

Each day flowed inexorably into another. The scientists met in conference rooms, the air thickened with smoke, chalk scraping on blackboards as they threaded their way through brain-numbing equations. Maddened by frustration, they found themselves trying to balance the keenest cutting edge of science against their own intuition, for they moved through a world where the impossible was reality.

The damned thing burned, and it couldn't.

Since the impossible was their lot, they struggled through the muck of chasing the impossible, and they found the miasma too thick for meaningful progress. It wasn't enough to seek complex answers when the questions themselves could be defined only in the most simplistic fashion. So they cooperated, and they struggled and fought with one another, and Dr. Kathy Farrel had her teams working around the clock to run every question, every proposal, every possibility through the computers. The computers kept coming up with the phrase they all came to hate: *insufficent data*.

Professor Owen Kimberly kept trying to herd his charges back to the basic questions, to the stark reality of what they faced and what they had to do to eliminate the threat of the blaze contained within the magnetic sheath. His task seemed as difficult as lighting the fusion fire, for these were men and women who had spent entire lifetimes working within clearly defined limits and with known quantities. Where unknowns existed in their work, they remained essentially theoretical and could be approached with the ease of a man settling into a comfortable armchair.

Not now. Most especially not now, because Kimberly had begun to "grasp the handle" of the beast that haunted them day and night.

"We're trying to isolate a factor," he explained to Angela one night, for Kimberly had discovered that trying to discuss the utterly complex with a person who thought in everyday terms was a help in his own attempts to understand the problem. Angela understood his terms and expressions just so long as Kimberly kept them within her limits of definition, and when he did this he could explain, provoke her questions, and seek answers within her limits of comprehension. She was sharp and intelligent, but her exposure to physics remained limited, and thus Owen was forced to speak *her* language and, to no small measure, clarify his own thinking.

So he told her in words squeezed down from the intricacies of equations that everything pointed to the X factor they sought to identify.

"We've got a fire burning. It *can't* burn because it's not burning fuel. By that I mean it's not getting any input we can measure. A star, Angie, is the result of millions and maybe billions of years of collecting dust and cosmic debris. As it collects, it gains mass and—"

"A self-contained celestial vacuum sweeper," she broke in.

"You amaze me, you really do—did you know that?" he told her. "You have a way of taking the absolutely complex and making it seem like a kitchen recipe."

She sniffed at the compliment. "Don't knock it, Owen. I'd like to see any of your prize brain cattle do a souffle."

"It's hardly the same thing."

"Isn't it? You're talking about primordial soup no matter how you look at it. It's all a matter of degree, Owen, dear."

He shook his head. "Can I go back to my star? I was saying that a star, a sun, results from a great mass of debris falling inward to a common center. It builds up enormous gravitational pressure, and this heats up the core until—"

"Until God lights His match," she slipped in quietly.

"That's as good a metaphor as any," he agreed, much to her pleasure. "Anyway, you've got radiant pressure pushing outward from the center, and gravity squeezing inward, and you've got balance. But the thing got its material from somewhere. All the star can do is burn its available fuel until finally it goes out. But there's always a balance."

"Like squeezing a rubber ball," Angela said. "So

long as you keep squeezing, you can condense the ball from hand pressure. When you let it go, the ball springs back to its original shape."

Kimberly nodded. "Very good. The missing ingredient is the energy. To keep the ball squeezed, *you're* supplying kinetic energy. Muscle power. But the muscles are part of the heat engine that makes up the human body. So we know where the energy comes from."

She snuggled closer to him on the living room couch. "But that doesn't fit for your microstar, does it."

She hadn't asked a question. Angela had made a statement as if she had lived with this thing for months. He pushed her gently from him. "What did you call it?" He'd heard her clearly, all right, but her choice of words—

"Microstar. That's what it is, isn't it? I mean, the way you've described it, Owen, it *can't* be anything else."

He scratched his chin in the sign she recognized. Something was stirring within him. It was the kind of agitation he lived with comfortably, for it meant that indirectly his mind was working on a solution.

"Owen, why can't it be a star? I mean, a *real* star."

"Because it lacks the mass."

"Who says so?"

"Dammit, Angie, that's obvious. It's—"

"Really? Aren't you the same man who likes to tell everyone about that time, oh, a couple of hundred years ago, when the French Academy of Science said the idea of rocks falling from the sky was total idiocy and that anyone who even sug-

gested this seriously should be banned from all
scientific circles? And now," she added smugly,
"we've known about meteorites for years, haven't
we?"

"But—"

"Those people, Owen, I mean, the ones in the
French academy, weren't they the leading scientists of the world in their time? And weren't they
so sure they were right because the whole idea
was illogical and crazy?"

"Yes, but it's not the same thing."

She sat cross-legged on the couch and called the
dog. Thor came to her side and lifted his head to
be scratched. "Owen, those pendulums you had
installed. What readings have you had with them?"

His look was sharp. "Why do you ask?"

"I've read your papers, Owen. I've typed them,
remember? And when you spend as much time
with them as I do,"—she shrugged—"some of it
rubs off. So maybe your pet flame *is* a star but on a
microcosmic scale. How long ago was the idea of a
neutron star impossible to believe? Who could
believe a star only six miles in diameter where a
sugar cube weighs a hundred million tons, or whatever silly figure you use? But you're as much at
home with neutron stars and pulsars—maybe they're
the same thing, I don't know that much about
it—and maybe what's burning over there in the
dome *is* a microstar. And if it can't keep burning
without fuel, as you call it, that only means you
can't measure what it's taking in, or eating, or
whatever.

"Owen, you put those pendulums there to see if
you'd get a change in their movement, right? Now,
then, if they do register that change, it's got to be

a slowing effect on the side away from the microstar. Yes, that's it," she said, as if she had closed out all argument. "It's a tiny black hole."

Everything she said had occurred to them, of course, but hearing Angela talk in this manner, almost diffident to the incredible danger—Angela argued with him that if the end were inevitable then there wasn't any use worrying about it, and they might as well keep working and enjoying everything they did until the last moment—placed a different perspective on his own thinking.

He jumped up so unexpectedly that the dog leaped to his feet, ready to defend them both from whatever it was Owen might have seen.

"Angie, would you mind putting on coffee? A big pot?" He didn't wait for an answer but went for the telephone, called Richard Clayton, and told him to come over right away. He asked him to bring Kathy Farrel with him.

Angela recognized the signs of an old-fashioned skull session and prepared sandwiches along with the coffee. Dr. Clayton, she remembered, would prefer tea, so she set water to boiling.

When Angela saw Clayton her impression was that he was wasting away to a ghostly reflection of his former self, and she was disturbed by the signs of shakiness in his hands. But whatever his physical problems were, Clayton's mind functioned as well, if not better, than ever before.

She sat with them, except for necessary trips to the kitchen, so she knew when some sort of break-through in decision-making, if nothing else—had been reached.

"I called the lab while you were on your way

here," Kimberly told their guests. "The pendulums have finally showed results."

"Both types?" Clayton's query was sharp but asked quietly.

Kimberly nodded. "Yes, both the metal and the wood. If only the metal had responded, I'd be inclined to distrust the readings. But the wood? It can't be any sort of electromagnetic field, of course. It's got to be gravitative in nature."

Kathy Farrel sat with both hands on the armrests of her chair. "You realize what you're saying, of course?"

"I do. And it's impossible. We have a specific gravitational field within an immense gravitational field."

"You're saying more than that," Clayton offered. "You're saying that something smaller than we can even see, were it not for the visible radiation, is overcoming the acceleration of the earth's gravitational field, aren't you?"

Kimberly glanced at Angela, then turned back to Clayton and Farrel. "I am."

Clayton sighed. "I can't say it's impossible. We threw out that word weeks ago." He sucked in air. "But that means the fusion fire—"

"Angie called it a microstar."

"Whatever," Clayton said. "You're saying it's exerting a force field—"

"No, Dick. I'm saying it has established, and is increasing, its own gravity field with every passing minute."

"Are you serious, Owen? You're trying to tell me we've got a black hole on a micro scale?"

Owen Kimberly leaned back in his chair. "Yes. That is what I'm saying."

"But we don't even have any ideas of the radius of a black hole! We—"

"Stop right there," Kimberly broke in. "You've answered whatever objections you might raise. Dimensionally we're blind when it comes to a totally collapsed star. We *think* we know how a black hole is formed. We have some evidence, we have a hell of a lot of theory, and until now it's been academic. . . ."

Angela listened with fascination mixed with the realization that what her husband of nine days was saying might well be the death knell of them all. Because if what he was describing *was* a black hole, no matter what its size or radius, he was talking about the most powerful force that existed anywhere in the universe. She listened closely to what he was saying. The room was silent except for his carefully selected conclusions.

"In its simplest form—and we have no choice but to accept events on the level that we're dealing with reality, no matter how bizarre—that fire, or flame, is functioning exactly in the same manner as a black hole, a totally collapsed star. And if this is so, then it must affect the space-time continuum. I know it all sounds mad, but when I was talking with the president—my God, it seems like a hundred years ago—I brought up this possibility. Talking with him, then, before I came down here, I was right at home with the theory because it *was* theory." He smiled at his own discomfiture. "But now that I've got to force myself to accept that it's reality, I have to fight to do it." He took a deep breath and plunged on.

"I have no choice but to accept what every ounce of logic and common sense fairly screams at me to reject. We are dealing with a black hole. It now exists on a microcosmic scale, but that scale means absolutely nothing. If it is indeed a black hole, then very soon it will go dark. There will be no visible radiation, but our readings in the X-ray and other lines should increase correspondingly."

He let it hang there, and no one spoke for several minutes. Each was being forced to wrestle with the monstrously impossible. They all knew of what Kimberly spoke. The tiny star existed because it had managed, in some way beyond their comprehension, beyond every physical law they knew, to rupture whatever veil existed between this and another universe, or dimension. It had drawn its mass through this rupture, but now it was growing. That was the meaning behind the change in swings of the pendulums Kimberly had ordered placed at different distances from the fire. The fact that the swing on the pendulum side to the fire had increased and had decreased on the opposite side, could mean only that a gravitational effect was being exerted.

Within the earth's field of gravity a tiny core, a gravitational field that mocked the mass of the planet, had leaped into existence. And it would grow.

"What happens if we shut down the force field?" Clayton asked abruptly, his frustration adding bite to his words. "If we just shut down the goddamned thing, cut off the flow to the bottle?"

They thought about that for a few moments. If suddenly they ended the force field within the vacuum bottle that was still containing the enormous temperatures and pressures—

"We would have on our hands," Kathy Farrel

said quietly, "a hydrogen bomb greater than anything we ever imagined. It would be in the very high gigaton yield, many billions of tons of explosive force or even trillions of tons. I don't know. At those energy levels, you'd get atmospheric blowout, and you would probably melt the earth's crust in the immediate vicinity, to say nothing of the earth shock and other effects. You'd—"

"Christ, it would be better to take that kind of punishment than to let this thing keep growing!" Clayton snapped, his voice near shouting. "I mean, Jesus, we'd take the blast and everything else, and we'd be over all this. We wouldn't face something getting worse every day until—" he sucked in air and forced his voice down—"until we have no hopes of doing *anything*."

They looked at Kimberly, who shook his head slowly. "It's not the solution. It may seem like it, but—"

"Why not?" demanded Clayton.

"Because it wouldn't do any good. I'm positive of that," Kimberly said with a conviction they knew they wouldn't dissuade. "In terms of our microstar— you'll forgive my accepting that description—you forget it has actually twisted, or warped, or whatever you want to call it, the space-time continuum. It doesn't depend, it never depended, upon the mass of the immediate vicinity to sustain itself. That may happen now, but in terms of the microstar being contained? While it's fed mass or energy or both? No, that's not it. The force field, the magnetic sheath, isn't keeping anything from getting *to* the microstar. I hate to admit this, but if that thing had any capacity for emotion, it would have utter and absolute contempt for everything that makes up this planet. It's a density, a mass beyond our conceiving, and the whole planet, I'm afraid, is only a fraction of the energy levels of the microstar. In not too much time from now, as I've said before, its inward acceleration will exceed light velocity, and it will go dark. From then on, our time remaining will be measured in days, or"—he shrugged—"perhaps hours."

He selected a sandwich from the tray on the coffee table, then bit down, unaware of what he was doing. "All our own force field is doing, really, is protecting us from the heat and pressure that's being radiated from the thing. If we shut down our own bottle, we would have absolutely no effect on the microstar, but we would, in turn, be exposing ourselves to the worst effects of the radiation spectrum."

Angela moved closer to Kimberly. "Owen, may I ask a question?" He nodded, and she went on. "You're saying, then, that the only real purpose right now of that vacuum bottle, and the magnetic force field, is to protect us from the—the star?"

"Yes, I'm afraid so."

"What would happen if the power source, or the magnetic bottle, itself, failed?"

The scientists looked at one another. The effect of Angela's words sank deeper and deeper into their thoughts, for they had never expressed the problem in quite the manner they had heard it through her questions. They had been so obsessed, and understandably so, with the need to understand the fusion fire that no one had bothered to say aloud just what Angela had presented in the form of her question.

What happens if the system breaks down?

"I'm afraid, Mrs. Kimberly—"

"Angela, please," she said to Clayton.

"Of course. Thank you. I'm afraid none of us would survive beyond the first few moments. It would be like being exposed—perhaps without the full blast wave—to the hard radiations of an exploding nuclear weapon."

"A radiation bath, in other words," she said quietly.

"In any words we might use," Clayton answered with a calmness he hadn't shown the entire night, "that's about it."

"Then we're twice as vulnerable as we imagined," Angela said.

"How do you mean that?" The question this time came from Kathy Farrel.

"Because if anything interferes with our electrical power system," replied Angela, "the magnetic bottle would shut down, the radiation would pour out, and we could never do anything about the microstar, could we? We couldn't even get near it, then."

The same thought occurred to the other three people in the room, almost at the same instant. *My God, she's right . . .*

They had no time to answer. The telephone rang, and Angela crossed the room to answer it. She listened for several moments, asked the other party to wait, then cupped the phone in her hand and turned to Kimberly.

"Owen, it's Michaelson, down at the lab. They've just had a call from the White House. The Russians will be here in the morning."

Kimberly was on his feet, glancing swiftly at

Clayton and Farrel. "At last," he breathed heavily. "At long last those damn fools are showing up."

He looked at Angela. "Is Tretyakov with them?"

She relayed the question, turned back, and nodded. "Everyone you asked for, Michaelson says—"

A shock ran through the floor, and Angela, thrown violently from her feet, fell against the wall. Owen had been standing, and he grasped the edge of the couch for support. The dog bared his teeth in an instinctive snarl at some unknown, unseen enemy. Dust drifted through the air, and the shock was gone as quickly as it came.

"An—an earthquake!" Kathy Farrel gasped.

Angela held out the phone to Owen, who took it from her as she ran upstairs to the children, the dog at her heels.

"Can you still hear me, Herb?" Owen asked.

A shaken Herb Michaelson spoke back at him. "Y-yes, Owen. What the hell was that? It felt like an earthquake!"

"It wasn't."

He said it so quickly, so easily, that Clayton and Farrel riveted their attention to him.

"Herb, I want you to keep this line open. Don't close it for a moment. Are you in the main control room? Good. I want you to look into the system and tell me what you see. What? Of course I know what I'm saying! Dammit, just do as you're told. Yes, yes, I'll keep the phone in my hand."

He looked up at the two scientists. "He's checking."

Kathy Farrel stood unsteadily. She looked at a crack in the wall nearest her. "Owen, you said—it wasn't an earthquake?"

"That's right."

"But—but how can you be so certain? You were right here when—"

"Shock effect. Shifting of pressures, Kathy. But nothing to do with crustal movement beneath us. It's started, that's all."

His calm was beyond belief. He seemed so sure of what he was saying.

Kathy gestured in confusion. "You asked Michaelson to make a visual check of the system, didn't you?"

"That's right."

"But—but what do you expect?"

"I'm afraid that he won't see a thing."

"I don't understand."

"If I'm right, Michaelson will no longer be able to see our star. It will have gone dark. That means, of course, that it's become a true black hole, that the force field of the star itself will be spinning, and as it continues to double its mass, to square its growth, it will be sending out sudden bursts of gravitational energy. In whatever space-time that damned thing exists, its surface acceleration is greater than the speed of light. We may be able to find some tachyon effects. Certainly we'll be looking for them for confirmation."

"Tachyons?" They hadn't heard Angela returning from the upstairs bedroom until she spoke. She came down the steps slowly. "I've never heard of them. I mean, what are they?"

"Particles that move only at velocities greater than light, my dear." Owen's sudden calm was a mystery to everyone save Angela. She understood. He had come to face the problem head-on.

"Yes, go ahead." He was again at the telephone. "Thank you, Herb. Yes, that's right. Set up the equipment as you've described it and make certain the Russians are brought to the lab the moment they arrive. Give them everything they want until I'm notified and can get there. Yes, thank you. You do that. Good night."

He hung up the telephone carefully, almost gingerly. They heard sirens wailing in the distance—fire trucks as well as police. People must be frightened. And with good reason, Kimberly thought. Then he looked up again at his wife.

"I've got to call the White House. Angie, would you do that for me, please? Top priority on the call. Oh, forgive me. Are Susan and Peter all right?"

"They're fine, Owen. Just frightened a bit. I left Thor with them." She descended the rest of the stairs. "Owen, have you looked at the time? It's four in the morning. I'm afraid the president—"

"I'm afraid he must hear from me at once, my dear," Kimberly said with care. "You see, the star has gone dark. Michaelson couldn't see a thing. Only—black."

13

Vasily Tretyakov was big, almost huge. Not tall, but even at five feet ten inches, he offered the impression of overwhelming strength, of wide-barreled massiveness. The feeling of brute strength was not in the least diminished by Tretyakov's dark business suit, for the jacket accentuated his broad shoulders and fitted tightly across his muscular back. He had a habit of standing wide-legged and looked as solid as a great tree trunk given the power to move at will. His face was broad, his eyes sharp and dark.

At this moment Vasily Tretyakov, a leading scientist of the famed Academy of the Soviet Union, stood in the center of the control room of Project Star Bright in the rolling hills of Cumberland, Tennessee. For long moments he held his wide-legged stance, his heavy fists against his hips, as he looked around the room at the engineers, technicians, and the scientists. Then he turned slowly, lifting his eyes to the second and third tiers of the control room, where more men and women stood. By the time he finished a complete circle, his piercing gaze had been directed at the more than eighty people who were present. Tretyakov stood center stage in a setting that would have warmed the heart of a dramatist. The immediate world in the domed control room consisted of row upon row of dials, gauges, controls, and panels, all flickering or aglow with lights of varied colors, with tape recorders going through their motions of impressing data on magnetic tape. It was a scenario of the mad scientist, and Vasily Tretyakov would have, on the surface, most aptly fit this description.

Those who watched him felt less his physical presence, awesome as it was, than they did his personality, for Tretyakov was a man of genius who spoke with either gentle tones or the bellow of a great bull. Visibly angry, he had been talking in a voice that had grown steadily louder until he had begun to shout, turning steadily, his arms flung wide, trying to reach, successfully as it turned out, everyone in the room who played his audience, including his own party that had accompanied him from the Soviet Union.

"Children playing with dynamite, every one of you!" he shouted. "Have none of you even understood the elemental forces? Are you all so blind! Are you so hungry for energy, so greedy for fame and your dollars, that you would not observe even the most basic rules of control? Of safety? You—"

His voice cut short as Owen Kimberly came into the control room. Behind Kimberly stood Richard Clayton, Kathy Farrel, and several other scientists. None of them moved, waiting instead for Kimberly to handle this Russian madman in their midst. Dr. Vasily Tretyakov was openly contemptuous of, and angry at, the Americans who ran the fusion research center, and he spared no words in venting his anger. Long minutes before Kimberly and his group had shown up, Dr. Lawrence Pound, white and shaken from the storm cast upon him by Tretyakov, had with final shreds of dignity abandoned the control center. The Russians had been at the center perhaps sixteen hours, during which time they had probed, queried, studied, and made swift calculations. They seemed to grow ever more agitated, and sharp words passed between them. More and more they had cast incredulous and then angry looks upon the Americans who explained, showed, and exposed whatever it was the Russians sought. Those had been the orders from Kimberly himself, and he was in turn backed by the White House.

Vasily Tretyakov gave no indication of gratitude that he had been treated not only with civility, but with naked honesty. He seemed to expect no less than absolute candor, and indeed he should have, because this had been promised him in the exchange between the leaders of the two countries. However, human ego being what it is, the Americans who felt the sting of his lash reacted predictably— they were defensive and ignored the fact that everything Tretyakov said was disastrously accurate.

The gist of his anger was that Project Star Bright was maniacal in its lack of controls of the unexpected. But the Americans already knew that and did not welcome the Russian pounding on their collective heads the bad news with which they had lived ever since Kimberly had come onto the scene. Now with the Russian standing in their midst,

Kimberly assumed a new role, that of the insider. He had come to Star Bright in much the same guise as the Russian, an outsider brought in to find a solution, and Kimberly had preceded his appearance, and followed it up, with his own scathing anger and contempt. Although he had been oblivious to it, he had been the object of much gossipy comment and resentment on the part of the larger body of technicians and scientists who comprised the working staff of Star Bright. That was not unexpected; this majority of personnel who bore no role in concept or decision making in the manner of bringing the fusion fire into existence still suffered the lash of Kimberly's wrath, his round-the-clock scheduling, his stark security measures, his vehemence and immediate sacking of anyone who fought the emergency re-scheduling.

Yet they could not fault the man for the reason he was there, nor could they dismiss the warnings he had made years before, and there was little argument that he might well be the last person, the only person, in the world who might extricate the planet from its final weeks of existence.

However, with problems increasing—the mobs collecting in the countryside, the inability of the scientists to combat or even to comprehend the awesome microstar, the insidious spread of fear—the staff did not need to listen to this bear of a Russian with *his* stinging tirade. It was just about enough to tip the scales to complete hopelessness. So when Professor Kimberly, who had been and remained an outsider, appeared in the control room, he instantly became the insider, the man who could deal with the Russian. The staff watched and listened as the two men came together on the main floor of the control room.

For several moments, Tretyakov appraised the man before him. They knew one another, if not personally, at least through papers presented in international scientific journals. Finally the Russian nodded slowly, extended his hand, and the two men greeted one another personally, although stiffly.

"I know of you, of course," Tretyakov said in a voice that was now calm, but sounded somewhat puzzled, as though he were searching his memory for something specific.

Then things fell into place. A smile appeared and grew slowly across his face. It was an overwhelming grin by the time he finished. "Aha! I am surprised to see you *here*. Years ago," he said, "you were the bright one in all this. We followed you closely. Then you left. The angry young man."

"As you say, that was years ago," Kimberly told him smoothly. "I was younger then, and so were you. The years have given me some wisdom. I hope they have done the same for you."

Tretyakov stared, for the moment taken aback. Then he laughed. "Good. You speak like a man."

He glanced about him. "But we should go right to the heart of this matter, no? All this is madness, Professor Kimberly. Madness, you understand? How you people could—"

But Kimberly had raised his hand to stop the flow of words. "Please, Dr. Tretyakov. You have been here long enough to find out what you needed to know. You have been left on your own, without interference or even without what could be prejudice on my part. That is why I left you alone with our control teams, why you haven't spoken with anyone else, especially Dr. Clayton. We did not wish to influence you or your people in any way. Making your own conclusions was vital."

Tretyakov's face had darkened, and his brow showed thick furrows. "That we have done," he said, not bothering to hide his sarcasm. "A nuclear war might be better than what is happening here."

The control teams had never heard Kimberly like this, and they listened with fascination. "That is a stupid remark," Kimberly answered at once. "Stupid because it has no basis in our science and because you know as well as anyone else what it would mean. Doctor, I'm going to be very blunt, as I believe you would want me to be."

"Good." That was all from Vasily Tretyakov.

"The last thing I want from you or your people is diatribes or accusations or anything else even remotely related to such talk. We are not here, and you were not invited, to criticize or to praise. Either you understand the purpose of your visit and work with us, or I suggest you and your party return immediately to your country."

Kimberly paused, trying to take the measure of the man before him. Tretyakov had thrust his hands into his jacket pockets, nearly tearing the material. His head was cocked slightly to one side as he studied the man talking to him. But he offered no word. He was a powerful man in his field, and he was perfectly capable, as Kimberly had judged, of completely separating his personal feelings from his professional needs.

"In short, Doctor," Kimberly went on, "we believe we need your assistance. By now you're completely aware of the problem we face?"

"Very clear, indeed, my dear Kimberly."

"So much the better. I am not unacquainted with your own fusion program in Vestyavich. So I am also aware that what happened here could just as well have taken place in *your* laboratories. It is neither fortunate nor unfortunate that this became our responsibility. But since the existence of the planet itself is now threatened, you have joined, willingly or not, into that responsibility, and we are asking for your help. I want to remind you that but for certain events in our laboratories or yours, you might be making this same speech to me in Vestyavich. Are we in accord with one another?"

You could never anticipate the Russians. A thick hand jerked from the right side pocket and was extended to Kimberly. "Your name is Owen, and mine is Vasily. Let us go to work."

"So you understand, my friend? We are running out of time in a way perhaps none of you expected? Your magnetic bottle, it is excellent, and it does its job most well. If it did not"—the big Russian hesitated—"none of you would be alive now. But your computer is wrong," he added, with a glance at Kathy Farrel, "when it reads to you that you have time to contain the energy inside the vacuum bottle."

Tretyakov was in comfortable dress. Gone was the business suit. He wore heavy slippers, his shirt was open at the throat, and his sleeves rolled up. He chain-smoked one harsh Russian cigarette after another, stubbing them out first in ash trays and then carelessly on the floor.

One wall of the room in which they had gathered was filled entirely with blackboards; chalk dust was everywhere. There were also direct programming inputs to the main computers as well as real-time readouts. It was, quite effectively, a brain-storming center.

The Russians had added a touch none of the Americans expected. Two men recorded everything that went on verbally, and another man and woman took direct notes, many of them in equations rather than words. At any moment that Tretyakov or the others wished to backtrack, they had almost immediate access to what had been said, and if they had committed to words an idea or thought that had special significance but had been passed over, it was available for recall at any time. Tretyakov explained that at the end of such sessions as theirs right now, he had his assistants prepare for him a concise summary of everything that had transpired. It was an effective system and one that Kimberly especially appreciated.

"Now, to the point at hand," continued Tretyakov. "The mistake is in assuming the energy from what you call the microstar would remain unchanged. We still understand no more than you this idea that we have a black hole, especially on such a microscale, but there is no time to play parlor games and talk for weeks. Whatever happened when your star goes dark, it is then that you have both the finite gravity field and a release of other energies. In not much longer time from now, Owen, the electromagnetic field will not hold back what is happening inside that bottle."

The Americans exchanged troubled glances. There was no triumph or anything of a personal nature in the remarks of Tretyakov or his staff.

There was only grim concern that everything the Russians said was true.

"What do you recommend, Vasily?"

"We must go out in teams with special equipment. We need more proof, too. We need to identify what is happening. It will take only a few hours, and then we will know what we need to do."

Kimberly and Tretyakov worked with several men from their own groups and sent out other teams. They went to distances measured with great precision from where the microstar burned in darkness. Each team, including those airborne in helicopters, then began to work back to the fusion blaze. And as each team advanced, shortening the distance, the special radiation instruments they carried began to register increasingly higher intensities.

Kimberly and Tretyakov were several hundred yards from the building, riding slowly in an elaborately equipped van, when Tretyakov motioned for a halt. He tapped the dials around him. "There is no doubt," he sighed. "I am afraid we were right. . . ."

The magnetic sheath was still containing the heat and pressure, still managing to draw it off in the evaporation system and generators, but entirely unexpected levels of radiation were ripping outward from the fusion fire. Streams of subatomic particles pulsed from the fire source. Gravity waves were building in strength, and the signs first indicated by the pendulums were becoming more and more noticeable in other ways. More than anything else, this troubled Kimberly and Tretyakov.

If the effects were being squared, then they would run out of time with a terrifying rush.

It was much the same as the old story of a man offering to work for a businessman at the rate of a penny a day for one month, just so long as each day's pay doubled the amount of the preceding day. At first glance it seemed that the man making the offer was a fool, but when the numbers began squaring, the effect was astounding. Starting at a penny for the first day, the progression was visible.

For his first day's work he earned a penny. The second day he made two cents. The third day's take was four cents. By the seventh day, he had earned the lordly sum of sixty-four cents. Of course, for the first week, his total earnings were only $1.27.

But counting only the wages for each day, and not running totals by adding each day to the prior time, by the eleventh day the man would be earning $10.24 for that day.

At the end of the second week, his wages would be $81.92—for that day only. And from that moment on the rise becomes astronomical. By the seventeenth day his daily pay has become $655.36, and by the end of the third week the wages for that day alone would come to $10,485.76.

On the twenty-fourth day the workman would earn $83,886.08, and by the end of the twenty-eighth day, he would earn $1,342,177.28 *for that day alone.*

On the last day of the month, thirty-one days after he started, his wages for one day's work would come to $10,737,418.24. There really isn't any need for him to total up the earnings for the month because the numbers have become meaningless.

In such a crude analogy, this is what so concerned the Russian scientists. Up until this moment, the magnetic sheath within the vacuum bottle had contained the outrushing energy. But not for much longer.

Within four days from this moment, exposure to the radiations within a thousand feet of the source would be hazardous to all living forms and dangerous to sensitive equipment, either rendering it useless for accurate readings or wrecking it altogether.

"There is no choice," Tretyakov concluded. "You must move everything back, all people and the equipment with which we work, to a minimum of one thousand feet from the microstar. By the way," he said smiling, "our little friend will start becoming visible in another twenty-four hours."

He laughed at Kimberly's raised brows. "No, no, my friend, there will be no change in the spectrum. But the rising energy levels will affect atmospheric atomic structure, even buildings and trees, anything within its reach. Such things will become unstable and begin to glow in the visible spectrum. Like a plasma, you see?"

Kimberly saw. That was all they needed, the extra touch to tip emotional balance—a world that began to glow visibly. The Russian found a source of amusement in Kimberly's somber reflections.

"It is an ironic touch, is it not, Owen? How many years did our people insist that all matter, organic and nonorganic, gives off a radiation? And how long were they ridiculed? Now, Kirlian photography is child's play. The leaves of trees glow beautifully, a man's hand is a wonder to behold, and even a rock gives off its strange electrical force. Now, well, we shall *all* be able to see such things without the photographic apparatus."

Tretyakov switched subjects abruptly. "Let me ask you something, my friend," he said, and the levity was gone from his voice. "Back home I know how we would handle this problem of moving back from the energy source; we tell people what to do, and it is done. But your system, ah!" He shook his head. "There will be no time for caucus, Owen Kimberly, and I fear your Dr. Pound has all the authority of—how would you call it?—a limp rag, I believe." He laid a powerful hand on Kimberly's arm. "If you do not mind the suggestion, call your leader in Washington. The president himself. You need harsh measures, Owen, and this calls for the military."

"The army's coming in tomorrow morning, Sam."

Sam Bruno looked up sharply at Kimberly's words. "Straight out, Professor. You unhappy with me?"

Kimberly would never cease to marvel at the sensitivity of human souls. "We're not talking about the same thing, Sam."

Bruno shrugged. "Maybe. And maybe you're right. We need more muscle. The National Guard isn't hacking it. Did you know that in the last three days we've killed over a hundred people trying to break in here?"

Kimberly was shocked, and he couldn't hide it. "*Killed* over a—Sam, what the hell is going on out there!"

"Well, you remember we talked about this El-Asid character. El-Asid, my foot. His real name is Vic Mattson, and the son of a bitch is a convicted army deserter. He's a wild-eyed, wild-haired, bible-thumping fanatic of the worst sort, and he's got this charisma or whatever they call it. The new Jesus, come to save the world from us, and—well, the rest of it's the same old crap. He stands on a hill outside the reservation in a long flowing robe and he's got the loudest damn speakers you ever heard. The people are listening to him pretty serious. We're getting bonzai charges, for Christ sakes—people loading themselves up with explosives and throwing their bodies against the barbed wire we've set up around this place."

Kimberly felt another wave of shock.

"You look surprised, Doc. Hell, we're sitting inside electrified fences, surrounded by land mines—the works. And still they try to come through to blow up this place. You hear that thunder yesterday?"

Kimberly motioned nervously. "Yes, yes, but I didn't pay much attention to it. Why?"

Bruno shifted in his seat and stuck a cigarette between his lips. "Because it wasn't thunder. This whole area is restricted to all planes. Any kind. Some nut tried to come through, I guess, and dive into the dome. Must have thought he was a kamikaze. Anyway, we're ringed with Hawk missiles, and we fired a brace—they're automatic, by the way—and we nailed him. The thunder was those things firing and the warheads going off."

Kimberly listened in silence. He must force the personal tragedies from his mind. "That's your job, Sam. Apparently you've been doing it far better than any of us realized."

"Save the compliments, Prof. I don't like killing

women and kids any more than you do. Tell me about the army."

Kimberly explained the studies of the Russians and what they had predicted. The army was being called in not so much for area security as for the need to have engineers and thousands of men working as a tightly disciplined force to move the equipment, construct barricades, and build a radiation shield. They would have access to all road-building and construction equipment anywhere in the area. Sam Bruno was to work in total cooperation with them.

Bruno rose to his feet and moved to the door. "Good enough. But I got a suggestion. You'd better get another twenty or thirty thousand troops in here, and if they're marines or paratroopers, ready to go with firefight capability, so much the better. Because from what I get from my own grapevine outside this Garden of Eden, Professor, something like a million or more people are going to start collecting around here, and we're going to be neck-deep in bodies." Bruno turned and left.

Kimberly found himself staring in stark disbelief, numb, at the door through which Bruno had disappeared. The picture Bruno had painted was of mass slaughter, of people impelled by naked terror to attack and destroy. And why not? If they had come to believe that if they did nothing then most certainly they would die, what did they have to lose by risking their lives in the attempts to preserve the future? But no matter how hard he tried, he found it impossible to accept a grotesque scene in which thousands of men, women, and children had been cut down by bullets and cannon shells, or napalm, flamethrowers, or—

God. He buried his face in his hands.
It did no good. The clock swept on.

Within three hours of Owen Kimberly's call to
President Arthur Whiteson, the army began rolling
through the gates of the Cumberland Reservation
of the Atomic Energy Commission. Immediately
they began the emergency transfer of equipment
away from the microstar that had begun to glow
again with an unholy radiance and to build an
enormous emergency radiation shield behind the
new perimeter. Trucks, graders, bulldozers by the
hundreds clanked, roared, and snorted through
every hour of the day and night, throwing up
earthen bulwarks and readying positions for thick
concrete barricades. This was the general shield.

Where the teams worked, where the computers
were housed, further barriers of steel-reinforced
concrete were punched into the earth. It was as
necessary to protect the main computer system,
which reduced years of brain-squeezing calculations to only minutes or seconds, as it was to
shield their own bodies.

The remainder of the military forces went through
their well-practiced motions of setting up defense
perimeters against those still on the outside. By
the end of the first day, Sam Bruno, representing
Kimberly, had called for an additional twenty thousand troops, as well as fleets of helicopters and fast
armored vehicles.

People were beginning to believe the end of the
world was near, and there was an angry tide of
anger burgeoning from fear and desperation. For
too many years, the people of the land had been
misled and lied to, so the soothing placations from

Washington, even those of a popular president, were swept aside in the mushrooming of fear.

The scientists knew that if they had any hope at all of extinguishing the fire, it would happen only if they could also protect the complex facilities of Star Bright from the mobs. Which spelled mass killings, for they had learned that nothing less, not even waves of choking gas, would stem the tide of people trying to destroy the project.

Lieutenant General George Sebastian, a tough veteran of the worst fighting in Vietnam, a man who had led shock troops in combat, who had killed then and hated every moment of that killing (and whose feelings earned him the respect of his troops who hated the war even more than he did), came in with yet another wave of armored forces. The earth trembled from the rumbling sounds of tanks, armored personnel carriers, roving groups of mobile trucks with quad-mounted machine guns and cannons, and the growing fleet of killer helicopters. What Sebastian hoped to do was to strike so swiftly and with such overwhelming effect at any attempt to penetrate the perimeter of Star Bright that the shock might stay the attempts of other people.

Sam Bruno, who attended to interior security, laughed harshly at the military officer. "General, you're forgetting the oldest saw of all," he told Sebastian. "There ain't a goddamnd thing you're gonna' do except to kill a hell of a lot of people and hope the eggheads can beat that nuclear rap behind us."

Sebastian, troubled, honestly torn by it all, gave the other man a questioning look. "We're talking about some awesome firepower, Mr. Bruno."

Sam Bruno snorted at him. "Don't you military geniuses ever learn? How the hell do you kill a dead man?"

"Owen, I am sorry to bother you at this time of the night." Vasily Tretyakov stood in Kimberly's doorway, flanked by two armed guards. Kimberly motioned him inside and waved off the Russian's apologies. He noticed that Tretyakov had thrown a coat over his pajamas, and his usual flourish of spirit was conspicuously absent.

"Here, in the living room," Kimberly offered.

Tretyakov grasped his arm. "The kitchen. May we have coffee? We have not slept, none of us, and—"

Angela came down the stairs, still tying her robe. She had heard part of the conversation, and guessed the rest. "I'll make the coffee," she told them, but the Russian remained in the kitchen doorway, then went directly to the table.

He spread notebooks on the surface and motioned Kimberly to his side. "Here," he said, his nerves taut. He was anxious to get to what had brought him here at this time. He tapped the paper, and Kimberly stared at a sheet of equations. "Do you see?" urged Tretyakov. "It is not a mistake we made before, but we—"

Kimberly looked up. "I can see it, Vasily. A critical underestimate."

Tretyakov nodded vigorously. "Exactly! I am glad we do not have to argue for hours because we have less time than we thought before." He cracked his thick knuckles. "I had thought to make a speech to you, Owen. You understand? How I must now break my security? Reveal certain things that—"

He cut himself short, took off his coat and tossed it carelessly over the back of a chair. "But how ridiculous, no?"

Kimberly lit a cigarette. "You're talking about the weapons program."

The Russian hesitated only a moment. "I would not have bothered with the words, but a lifetime of being careful is a habit very difficult to break. Yes, yes, the weapons. Especially those we explode in yield of three gigaton."

Kimberly shook his head slowly. "That high? I'm surprised, Vasily. Even your people wouldn't—"

"Never mind. They did. It is most important *now. . . .*"

Not until Vasily began talking did Owen Kimberly, as well as Angela, come to understand just how closely the world had been on the brink of savage destruction for years, not from an accident, but from a hard drive within the hierarchy of the Soviet government to strike at the United States with a hammering first blow. The plan called for no more than a dozen weapons, each one equal in explosive force to three billion tons of TNT, and carefully spaced—four deep within the ground, three low air bursts, and five, acting as starbombs, at a height of a hundred and thirty miles. Their combined effect, timed carefully, would have destroyed the country as an entity, and in a single stroke—because of an enormous "punch" of electromagnetic force—rendered useless the guidance and computer mechanisms of the missiles of the United States.

Vasily Tretyakov did not delve into the reasons why such a blow had not been struck. That would come later, if there was to be a later. Right now,

Tretyakov insisted, what mattered was what they had learned in the test of their three-gigaton starbomb. When a certain energy level was surpassed in the implosion-explosion sequences of such a weapon, there appeared a flood of radiations never before known and totally unexpected by the Russian scientists involved in the weapons test.

The radiations were so incredible, and of a nature so wholly unanticipated, that a whole new research program had been launched to study them, and Tretyakov had been named director.

"I know," he said slowly, "it is difficult to believe, but we have time warp while the bomb is still exploding. Certain instruments, we use cesium decay timing systems as you do, indicated different times in areas from the point of greatest force, the implosion center. Time, Owen, time itself was changed. I am not bothering with talk between us of neutron stars and black holes, but tonight, only hours ago, we determined that the same effect is taking place here, now.

"You understand, Owen? There are certain radiations from your microstar that will make fun of the magnetic sheath, as you call it. The magnetic field, the bottle, the earth, the steel, and the concrete, they are all like fog, no? We are no more to such radiations than this whole planet is to a neutrino!"

The neutrino was a mysterious but real neutral particle with no known mass, without an electrical charge, moving at the speed of light. The thing could travel through fifty light years of solid lead without slowing down. To the neutrino, the concept of mass or density did not exist. It was affected only by force fields.

Kimberly understood what Tretyakov was trying

to drive home to him. There would be radiations streaming from the microstar because of time warps, or whatever, and the shielding of earth and concrete and steel would be no more than the thinnest wisps of fog to such radiations—just as cosmic rays streaming down from deep space whip through the entire earth as if it never existed.

"But—"

Tretyakov had anticipated the question. "No, there is no problem to *us*, to the people, from the direct radiation. Not the same as from ionizing radiation of X-rays or what we get from bombs. But moving through earth and atmosphere, my friend Owen, we will find ionization effects like nothing either of us has ever known before. They will be beautiful and frightening, but they are not important. What may happen, what we believe must happen, is that the ionization effect will produce an electrostatic field—a thunderstorm at its worst, only it will be *all* an electrical field and maybe a thousand times worse than anything we know!"

Owen Kimberly needed no further explanations. Vasily Tretyakov was devastatingly correct in his latest calculations. Once those radiations streamed from the microstar and created their own ionization of the atmosphere, the research center and surrounding countryside would exist within the core of something worse than a thunderstorm—a tornado of naked electrical force. They discussed the dangers and the Russian offered a solution.

The Soviets had been working on a project to deflect the explosive outpouring of radiation from air bursts of nuclear weapons; it would serve as a protective system for their cities and critical targets. What they had accomplished had a grim new meaning—it just might work against the radiations from the microstar.

"There is no way to stop such energies," Tretyakov emphasized, aware that Kimberly already knew this fact. But he had to say it all, to keep his continuity. "If we can place a ring of force-field generators in series outward from the source of the radiations—well, a dam does not stop water, but holds it or diverts it. So it is with these generators. They can deflect the radiations in a curve we anticipate, and then we twist it upwards, you see? So it moves horizontal to the earth only for a short distance and then it goes up, nearly perpendicular to the horizon."

"How long will it hold?" Kimberly asked after a long silence.

"You tell me how long your baby star lasts before it destroys us, and I will answer your question."

He drank his coffee, held out his cup for more, then patted Angela gently on the hand. She was constantly amazed by Tretyakov and his mixture of overwhelming strength and moments of gentleness.

"What difference?" Tretyakov shot at Kimberly. "It lasts until it break down, no? And we hope we are right."

"And pray," Angela said quietly.

Vasily Tretyakov leaned back in his chair. "*You* pray. You are a good woman. I like you. If I pray, it will be wasted as I do not believe in praying."

He grinned at Kimberly and pounded him on the shoulder. "See? As you say, we have your woman pray, and we will cover all bets."

Kimberly felt his skin smart beneath his pajamas. "How long will it take to build the generators?"

"My people work with yours. Eighteen hours, maybe, if nobody stops."

"They won't. Have you a list of what we need?"

Tretyakov waved a sheet before him. "All on here."

Kimberly studied it for several moments. "We can do it. I think it would be wise if I called the president. What we don't have here can be flown in immediately."

"However you think is right. Woman, you maybe make breakfast? The problem is solved. I am hungry."

They looked at him in wonder and then burst out laughing. And in those moments, pajama-clad and disheveled, they became fast friends.

14

There is a world men have never seen. Our planet is the crux of a fantastic energy vortex sweeping wildly into space and in captured orbits about the earth. Except for moments when the aurora borealis shimmers into ghostly being through the electrical fields that form a carpet beneath which we live, we never see our world as an enormous spinning electromagnet that weaves intricate energy patterns of stunning beauty. Energetic particles bound and swirl all about us. Radiant waves and bands sweep and rush from the surface into space and race back again. It is energy on a scale so monumental it seems impossible it can exist about us without being seen. But the human eye cannot see such energy and its effects. We are bound to see within only a small fraction of the energy spectrum, and most of our lives are spent in sad blindness to such beauty.

Earth is the densest of all worlds in this solar system. It rotates with great speed, a thousand miles an hour along the equator. These two features, density and speed, have made of our planet a most extraordinary magnet, the forces whirling outward being so great they create a massive screen that interacts with energy from the sun and that streams toward us from distant exploding stars and heaving galaxies.

If we could see, as instruments do across the spectrum, we would find, fifty thousand miles outward from the earth, in the direction of the sun, a great, glowing band of blue-white light, so intense as to resemble the curving edge of an incredible mirror glowing along its surfaces and from within its own substance. This is our planetary shock wave that defends us against terrible forces smashing at us from the sun; it is a line of battle between the earth's magnetic field and the continuous, tremendous tidal wave of the stellar wind from our sun.

Forty thousand miles out is the second line of demarcation called the magnetopause, the edges of which glow a dazzling yellow-gold, a celestial fire that flames along the surface of a royal purple fire. Still closer to earth is the magnetosphere, a force field gripping this planet in a shield of "radiation armor." Here the colors ripple and shimmer as the intensity of energy from the sun waxes and wanes. And when the sun erupts with violent storms and its debris sallies out toward our planet, space churns with a vast interplay of blazing energies that show their enormous power in the form of a vast bowl of coruscating, brilliant color within which our planet is no more than a dense spinning marble.

Now the invisible waves of energy began to emerge from that place beyond sight. . . .

*   *   *

Within nineteen hours of starting the absolute priority effort, the circular system of generators was completed. Vehicles with heavy armor protected heavily-suited men who laid out shielded cables behind them. Helicopters took over where trucks or tanks could not move. When the grid network was laid down, every detail monitored by Tretyakov and the other Russians, and the initial tests were completed, all those participating knew a moment of unexpected triumph. The system to bend, to deflect the savage radiations, needed energy far beyond the capacity of local current and there had been instant panic when this realization had struck home. Just as quickly, however, they understood the irony of the moment. The microstar was still powering the electrical generators of the fusion system, and they could draw limitless energy from the very source that threatened their destruction.

They *felt* the energy release almost as quickly as the system went active, for it was a sound beyond human reach, and it ground through the human body with a physical effect, a deep groaning bass that resonated along the bones and through the skull. People reacted in different ways. Some seemed to feel or sense what they called an ethereal music, others winced as their eyes seemed to twist in their sockets. It was an experience that ran a wide and wild gamut of human reaction, creating joy and despair and to some even a oneness with the energy they might attribute to God.

Such was the stance of Dr. Lawrence Pound, who found in the visible appearance a true sign of the Lord playing His celestial score.

"There is no doubt any longer," he announced to a crowd assembled about him as the zones of energy began to take shape before their eyes. "If the good Lord ever wanted us to see His glory as He must know it, then this is the place and the shape chosen by Him and no other. It is the glory exposed to us all, the splendor of heaven itself. It is His test of our faith in Him!"

And with those words, Dr. Lawrence Pound, Director of Project Star Bright, fell to his knees and spread wide his arms as, smiling beatifically, he raised his face to what he believed were the very heavens becoming visible.

It was difficult for many to dispute what Lawrence Pound saw, felt, and said, for here was no vision restricted to the sight of only one man.

Suddenly, all men were able to see the magical sight of the heretofore invisible radiations that had always resonated in tune with the universe. As the radiations poured outward from the flaming black star and were deflected by the energy raised from the ring of force-field generators, they moved upward in a bending path that slowly but inevitably began to take shape before the eyes of the awed spectators.

There came into being a spiraling upward funnel that shone and glistened during the day and glowed eerily blue at night. It was a funnel, or a tunneled vortex more than a thousand feet in diameter at its base, a tornado of pure seething subatomic forces and naked electricity. It defied anything ever seen before by man. It was more a religious experience for most than recognition of material force.

It was no tornado, of course, and those with experience in desert country soon termed it for what it resembled most of all—although on a vastly grander scale—a dust devil, a whirling tornado shape that rose from the ground to reach upwards. Only this was of elemental force, and it began its existence within the ring of generators, a thousand feet across, and expanded as it rose, so that by the time it was ten miles high, it was a mile in diameter, above which it spread even more rapidly until it seemed to flower across the upper reaches of the planet.

Which, indeed, was the case. The higher the dust devil of plasma rose, the weaker became its own force, and the more it reacted to and was disturbed by the enormous magnetic field of the planet, by the radiation belts frozen in orbit, and by the ever-turbulent solar hurricanes that thundered earthward from the sun. The higher it rose the more violent became its colors until it raged silently through the full spectrum and made a mockery of the greatest auroras ever known.

Had it not represented the vanguard of hell itself it would have been regarded as the most beautiful and ethereal sight ever known to man— vast sheets of softly undulating folds of pure energy, great shimmering curtains glowing upward and outward, as if someone had tapped the silent orchestration of the pure energies that might flow from angels.

But there was nothing angelic here. Those who had joined ranks against the murderous effect of the microstar looked away from the glowing heavens to concentrate on the task of saving the world from utter destruction.

Within hours, there were other effects. Electrostatic forces set up a spattering crackle in the air, the sound of high-tension wires magnified a hundredfold. The air hummed with electrical energy, and the upreaching funnel destroyed all radio transmission except that of the highest frequencies. The air within reach of the funnel was rendered lethal for any flying creature, whether it be plane or bird. As the hours passed, the funnel became more intense and its visibleness increased, so that even in direct, bright sunlight it could be seen in every direction for hundreds of miles.

It terrified the human race.

Temporary measures are never more than that. The combined efforts of the Americans and Russians— and they understood this only too well—had done nothing more than to delay the final act. Time was running out. Doubt no longer existed, even if true understanding lay beyond the scientists, that the black microstar was a pinhole between universes, one of this Time and the other of some unimaginable Elsewhen.

Time was slipping away from them, and it had become a cruel joke, a final jab of irony at its ultimate, for where the microstar raged there was no time.

The instruments surrounding the vortex were showing changes the scientists could not ignore and about which there could be no error. What was impossible was patently true. The early calculations of Professor Owen Kimberly, conceived as an exercise in scientific speculation, had found their way into their midst.

A penny a day doubled every day . . .

The black microstar was increasing its mass steadily, and it began to twist gravity about itself. The microstar had begun to sink into the crust of the planet.

15

No room was left for levity. Every move of the
scientists was grim, calculated, imperative beyond
anything they had ever known before. When they
met their eyes appeared gaunt, and the men's
faces were covered with stubble because there had
been no time for shaving. They ate in fits and
starts, living on coffee, gulping pills or capsules to
keep them moving.

"We can't do any more goddamned research,"
Kimberly announced, confirming in words what
they all knew. "We've got to work toward the
solution, to putting that damned thing out. Nothing else matters, nothing else will be tolerated."

Vasily Tretyakov made a move to interrupt, but
Kimberly motioned him to wait.

"I have simply got to make this so clear there's
no room for any misunderstanding. I don't want to
hear a thing from anyone except for proposals as to
how to kill that fire. I don't care if you want to use
water or bricks or a hydrogen bomb. I don't care

how exotic or crazy it might be. We need hard ideas, and no matter how weird it sounds, let's have it. Just so long as it doesn't take any time between coming up with the idea and trying to execute it."

He broke in on his own words, stubbing a cigarette into an ashtray. His movements were clumsy, his coordination so bad that he burned the end of a finger and never realized it. Kimberly had become a chain smoker. He'd never done that before. But worry, frustration, lack of sleep, and grabbing food on the run, had all taken their toll. His voice was hoarse and scratchy. He reached for a glass of water and quickly drank it.

"Dammit, I don't mean to sound like I'm faulting anybody here," he went on, his struggle for self-control apparent to them all. "I haven't come up with any ideas myself."

He looked at Tretyakov. "What was it, Vasily?"

The Russian shifted in his seat. "I want to report," he said, his voice rumbling, "that we have set up a direct link between your computers here and ours in Vestyavich. It may help." He shrugged, a physical movement they shared. "I do not know, of course, but—"

"You have a team assigned to work with Farrel?"

Tretyakov nodded. "Of course."

"Good. That will give us whatever's stored in your memory banks."

He turned to the woman who ran their computers. "Kathy, what's your move now?"

"We're trying everything possible," she said, her own voice dull with fatigue. "Plus something new. We're linked with the heuristics systems at the National Security Agency."

She glanced about the room. "So there's no mistaking what I mean, that's roughly a 'hunch' system. It won't reject any input on the basis of insufficient data. Whatever problem we give to it will be considered on the basis of all possibilities, and the most likely answer, considering everything, is issued. If anybody here comes up with something that needs programming, we have teams standing by at all times. The NSA systems have been cleared from all work except what they receive from us."

She didn't say more, which meant that everything they'd tried so far had come up a big fat zero.

Kimberly reached into his attaché case on the floor by his chair. As he did so the room shifted, and he tumbled from the chair, sprawling on the floor. Several people tried to reach him but were helpless from the same effects. The earth shocks were more frequent now, but they weren't those one experienced in an earthquake.

A quake rolls the surface or heaves it about. This was different. There was a sensation of being pulled. The gravitational bending, of course. Everything was being twisted out of shape. The soil beneath them was starting to shift. Water in underground rivers was diverting because of the strange pressures and deformation. Large buildings with steel structures had taken on a life of their own—the electromagnetic effect pulling even more strongly on metal. The grid was working, but now it strained to its utmost, and the microstar was gaining in mass and increasing its energy release. Even metal fillings in teeth were affected. Headaches had become stabbing pains grinding through jawbones and skulls.

At night it was worse. Vasily Tretyakov was right. Everything had taken on a glowing pulse of electrical life. Metal glowed blue, other objects seemed to shimmer.

They were getting waves of infrasound, a deep bass too low for the human ear to detect. The waves, however, could be picked up by the body. It was an effect long familiar to scientists, for infrasound was an acoustic signature that scientific instruments could detect from faraway thunderstorms. Those came and went, but what took place now stayed, rumbling through mood-shattering waves, even if no one *heard* the sound. But people reacted predictably—sudden rages, fits of depression, even moments of hysteria that struck without warning.

One day, Kathy Farrel was knocked senseless by a man at the computer banks. His input was rejected by the computer because of faulty data. He stared quietly at the paper, turned suddenly, and struck out at the person nearest to him. The blow caught Farrel on the side of her head and hurled her to the floor. Fortunately, Vasily Tretyakov was nearby, and he understood what had happened. Sighing, he reluctantly raised a huge hand and sharply cuffed the man along the back of his neck. He fell like a stone.

Vasily looked up at the people watching. "I am sorry," he said in his rumbling voice, "but—"

Another woman was already by Kathy Farrel's side, helping her up. "You saved her from much worse," she told the Russian. "Thanks."

Tretyakov had become immensely popular with the American team. Unfortunately, there had been no time before, and there was less now, for relationships to develop between people. No one knew who might flare up suddenly, and for what reason. The pressure of failure, the microstar that had become a horrible malignancy, the infrasound, the increasing gravitational twisting, all these strained relationships to the utmost.

One of their best computer programmers went berserk on the way to work. He drove his car at full speed into a house, killing himself and four people in the building. They didn't bother to find out the medical definition of why he'd done it. There wasn't time, there wasn't the energy, and no one cared.

The pinhole in time gnawed at them from without and within. They knew it increased every moment in mass and in effect. What could alter the surface of space-time could be no more than moments away from crushing them all.

It was the seeming contempt of the microstar—for there was no way they could consider the microstar without attaching a personality identification—that unbalanced them more than any other effect. A contempt measured in hopelessness and frustration. The scientific team was in danger of coming apart at the seams.

Which most of the world was actually doing. . . .

The physical effects were by now astounding, visible for thousands of miles in every direction. There was no hope in denying the danger, in trying to smooth over the imminence of utter destruction, by claiming some exotic electrical or magnetic research program was under way. The gloss of public relations coverup had long since worn away, and the nightmare beneath had emerged fullblown, hideous reality and all, and it raked at the human psyche.

The great blue funnel had increased enormously in size and in effects. It was much brighter than before, and even during the day it outshone the sun. At night it was a twisting-upward tornado of dazzling lights and colors, scrabbling at the human eye that tried to define its shape and never could. The visual, unfortunately, had been joined by a sonic effect that climbed well above the infrasound levels.

From the heavenly funnel there radiated a deep humming sound, a buzzsaw that crawled within the skull and scraped with jagged edges at the backs of the eyeballs, bringing on flash migraines that resulted in screaming agony, then disappeared and returned again without warning. Its effect was teeth-grinding and inescapable day or night, for it wandered up and down a scale of frequencies that seemed calculated to irritate and inflame every human emotion.

In addition, the electrostatic fields of the funnel had made of the atmosphere a sea of swirling charges. Positive and negative fields abounded as if in the midst of the most powerful thunderstorms ever known, and the results came in the form of lightning that ripped and slashed the air day and night.

Not since the birth of the planet had such lightning been known. It was as if primal forces had been cast loose, as if bolts of energy that helped create the world were back again, striding across the countryside in great leaps and bounds, juggernaut steps that shook heaven and earth together. There was no surcease from the raw energy. Every kind of lightning bolt imaginable danced wildly in the skies even where there were no clouds. The lightning roared and thundered between the air and the ground, and the countryside became pitted with areas where it had struck. Fires leaped up where the massive bolts struck without warning. To the terrified public, the lightning was another manifestation of the "satanic forces" being unleashed by the madmen of Project Star Bright.

There was no surcease from its effect; it struck with the force of sonic booms. There was no rest, no escape, and what had been awesome, even frightening, had reached a level where no one ever knew when he might be struck directly.

This was no *threat*—this was reality, and few people any longer doubted that they were witness to and participants in the final beginning of the end. There had been long moments before of the threatened end of the world—comets in the skies, earthquakes, exploding volcanic islands, tidal waves, prophets with the magic of sliding their warnings like knife blades between ribs—but none of these had been accompanied by the physical presence, the overpowering effect of elemental forces now running amuck. The towering funnel, twisting and writhing slowly, seemed alive as it extended its effect. The aurora swept from one pole of the earth to the other and girdled the planet along the equator with rich, striking, intense colors that were constantly shifting, kaleidoscopic to the point of visual madness. To many people this aurora encircling the planet was the unmistakable gossamer signature of energy gathering strength for its final blow upon the world of man.

These were the more impressive effects, but

they were by no means the signs of greatest danger, at least not to the scientists who understood all too well the meaning of force and energy, its cause and above all its effect. The tight little band of scientists, on whose shoulders rested the survival of the world, were much more concerned with other signs.

In every direction from the pinpoint that had ripped its hole between universes of time, there grew a tidal effect of gravity unknown to them. As Kimberly noted with not-so-subtle irony to his Russian companion, "All this is the dream of every scientist. We've always wanted to know what stuff makes up the universe, matter, and energy, and how it all came about. *Now* we're finding out, but in a fashion we never dreamed of or wanted."

Tretyakov grinned crookedly at him. "Are you scientist or philosopher, friend Owen?"

Kimberly scratched a stubbled chin. "Both, I guess."

Tretyakov surprised him with a massive hand slamming the table at which they sat. "Bah! You are a man, not a snickering fanatic! You know what a man is, Kimberly?" He didn't wait for an answer, "The end of the world looks us in the eye, and if we are men, we spit right back. We—"

"You pass it off rather lightly," Kimberly protested.

But it was a protest without rancor, for Tretyakov had turned out to be the most amazing man Kimberly or anyone else in Star Bright had ever encountered. The huge bear of a man, brilliant, volatile, powerful, had been a bedrock of patience and reserve throughout the worst nightmares. Nothing fazed him, nothing ruffled his composure. As the men and women of the team began to deteriorate, succumbing to their own emotional fears and nightmares, Tretyakov, and Kimberly with him, seemed to grow in strength, each man shouldering the burden of their fellow scientists.

Angela spent most of her hours now with Kimberly. She had made the decision on her own to return her children to Colorado where they would be with their grandparents. She had done this not so much for the safety of the children, but because she could not spare a moment from working with Kimberly. Parental love notwithstanding, Angela had never lost her own faith in Owen to prevent, even if at the last possible instant, the ultimate cataclysm. Were Susan and Peter still with them, they could not avoid being distractions, for Angela constantly feared for their safety in the crackling maelstrom always raging in their midst. Their best chance was in her helping Owen, in always being at his side, making sure he ate and drank to keep up his strength. He had slipped into total obsession with the black star and what he hoped would be its destruction at his hands, and he knew nothing of his personal wants and needs. Angela had become more than his alter ego; she steered him through the hours of day and night.

At the same time, she had joined with him in the cerebral sense, and Kimberly's thoughts flowed to her without hesitation. She was his sounding board, she made careful notes of everything he said, even when he was in a mild delirium of exhaustion, for she knew a single remark might have overwhelming consequences if it could be captured.

Angela watched an extraordinary relationship develop between Owen and Vasily Tretyakov. As scientists, Vasily and Owen were fast and strong brothers beneath the skin, but they had also gained a marvelous meeting of two souls, and between the two flowed a respect and admiration seldom achieved by any two people. There existed no barrier between the two, and Angela was pleased and grateful that Vasily Tretyakov had enveloped her within his sphere of friendship with her husband.

When Vasily had almost shouted that men must spit in the eye of impending total destruction, she felt vaguely disturbed. She agreed with Owen that Vasily did, indeed, pass it off "rather lightly," and she told him so.

His response was to rest his heavy hand gently on her shoulder. "Angie, woman, you are missing the point of all this. You believe in what you call the grand design of the universe?"

She hesitated for a moment. His "grand design" could so easily be the equal of her own theological beliefs, only couched in different terms. Finally she nodded. "Of course I do. You know that."

He looked her directly in the eye. "Then, little one, why are you fighting what is inevitable?"

She had vague misgivings that the Russian was leading her down some favorite primrose path of his own making. "Inevitable?" she echoed. "I don't understand, Vasily."

"Hah! You do not talk so well with your God, maybe. Do you ever think about nova in the sky, Angie? You ever think that every time a star explodes, maybe a whole solar system full of nice people like you and Owen, and"—he grinned impishly —"if they are lucky, even like *me*, are destroyed all and one and in an instant? If your God is so busy with making worlds and people, then he is also as busy burning them up and blowing up one after the other. How do we know that the same thing happening here is not also happening out there, hey?"

Kimberly scratched behind his ear. "Interesting point, but moot," he half agreed.

"Moot, shmoot!" Tretyakov bellowed. "You are missing the whole point of this. Angie, you are forgetting that all of us from the moment of birth are destined to die. This is so, right? So all that is happening is that we are maybe speeding up the process. If not this crazy black star your husband made, maybe the sun would move through a dust cloud. If the sun should hiccup, the earth would die from a sunburn that you could never imagine. If the sun calms down even a little bit, then the earth will freeze, but maybe some people could survive in deep caverns with nuclear reactors for few hundred years. But all this is not the point," he repeated. "We are intelligent creatures. We *understand* sun and energy and life, and we are a miracle like no other. So what happens around us now is beautiful, you understand? Beautiful! Because if we win, if we blow out Kimberly's star like a candle on a birthday cake, we are given a wonderful thing. We will know about time, we will understand how to twist and to untwist, and maybe even time travel is on our hands. Not so long ago, the idea of flying like bird was crazy. Now we fly where birds cannot even imagine. That close we are to understanding time." He took a deep breath and became calm. "It is worth the risk. I hope you understand this, Angie. Owen, he understands, even if he doesn't talk about this very much. But he knows, *I* know. It is all worth the gamble. If we are wrong"—his massive shrug conveyed with absolute clarity his contempt for death—"then all we do is die sooner than we should die anyway, which is little loss." He grinned at Angie.

"You know something? Maybe there is a God, whatever and wherever. Maybe. I don't know, and you don't know, but you are a believer. Maybe all this is a test, you think? And if we fail the test, why, your God is generous, no? And—"

Just then the floor shifted beneath them, and they lost their balance. By now they were no longer taken by surprise when the floor shifted or buckled, but they could never prevent the momentary fear that the movement of the earth would cause buildings to fall, crushing the inhabitants with tumbling beams or bricks. Coughing and choking, Owen, Angela, and Vasily Tretyakov picked themselves up from a dusty floor, and saw that the floor now rested at an angle.

"One thing is sure," spat Tretyakov, clearing his mouth of dust. "Whoever this God of yours is, He is making the test tougher." He grasped Kimberly by the arm. "Come. I have an idea. This last shock rattled my brain. Good."

The situation kept getting worse. Underground rivers were being bent from their course, the crust itself was deforming. For miles in every direction buildings and other structures began to lean inward to a common center. Trees bent in, buildings began to twist on their foundations, river banks crumbled. The effect was insidious and frightening and steadily worsening.

An invisible whirlpool of gravity seemed to

weaken the cloth on which things stood so that they fell inward. Hold a large napkin, stretch it taut, then place a heavy object in the center, and then another and another. Whatever else had been on that napkin must begin to lean in and to fall toward the center.

Thermal radiation was increasing. Every available ounce of power was going into the huge grid to deflect the subatomic radiations from the black star. Kathy Farrel reported they must have additional cooling capacity for the computers or they would stop functioning. The army rushed in huge refrigeration units operated by mobile gasoline-run generators. The computers stayed cool, but for how long no one would guess.

But they could do almost nothing against the growing tide, the whirlpools, of electromagetic energy pulsing through the earth and the air, making a hash of the computer memory banks, destroying their usefulness.

Time kept moving more and more swiftly. In the waning hours, Kathy Farrel, with Richard Clayton by her side, stood by the computer and read the dire results of their immediate studies.

They went directly to Kimberly and Tretyakov, and they broke the news without preamble.

Kathy licked dry lips. "There's no doubt. The effects are squaring, and—"

"Speak words with meaning," Tretyakov rumbled at her.

She glanced at Dick Clayton and took a deep breath.

"We have only eighty-four hours left."

16

Dr. Lawrence Pound felt his heart beating madly, an erratic pulsation that at any other time would have frightened him into insensibility. Not now, for he seemed to understand the sudden fibrillation came not from any physiological weakness, but rather from the surging moods he felt. Could there be any doubt left? Could any sane human being doubt any longer this ultimate sign in the heavens? The angels themselves must have been dispatched by God for this glorious presentation to man.

"Again, again, please!" he begged in a half-formed whisper from his quivering lips. "Please show us again, O Lord," and he kept his eyes riveted to the skies that for so many weeks had not known darkness.

His plea was answered. Or so he chose to believe, as perhaps did many others.

They could not have imagined the incredible sight. And even when they saw it again, they did not try to comprehend.

It was enough to see it happen. . . .

The blue funnel, howling with growing energy, had stretched higher and wider. It swept upward and mixed with the electrical atmosphere of the planet, then spread still higher to answer the pull and tugs of the radiation bands that orbit the earth. It twisted and ripped zones of radiation, and it struggled to find new outlets.

Time passed, and the celestial bodies moved in their orbits. The moon rose higher and higher over the horizon. It seemed the funnel of shrieking energy was pointing at the moon a quarter million miles distant.

Which it was. Unseen by human eyes, the thin trickles of electrostatic energy reached higher and higher, drawn by the moon. Like the invisible streamers that precede the shocking roar of a lighting bolt from a cloud to the surface of the earth, clouds of electrons swept through space, drawn by lunar attraction, and the thin clouds made of the same elements as pre-lightning streamers within our atmosphere, became thicker and stronger. The charges built higher and higher until the last resistance was overcome, and the electrical energy, dammed and pent up by natural barriers and the earth's own enormous field, ripped loose.

A lightning bolt, inconceivable in its fury, smashed away from the earth and tore into the surface of the moon. It was a blow of which man had never dreamed, and the instruments left on the lunar surface years before by the men who had flown in Apollo to the moon sent back radioed messages of the awesome energy release. Quakes hammered the moon, pealing like enormous bells through its rocky structure. A dust cloud rose miles high above the moon and helped build still more electrostatic energy.

The bolt struck again and again, and then a charge from the moon ripped earthward, and the dark heavens between earth and moon filled with a terrifying display.

The hammer of Thor . . .

A message from Satan . . .

Star Bright.

Because of who he was and the identification he carried as the project director of Star Bright, Dr. Lawrence Pound was able to pass through the heavily guarded gates, through the barbed wire, and through six different military checkpoints. The guards judged him to be a raving maniac, wild-eyed, hair disheveled, spittle on the corners of his mouth, but there was no doubting he was Dr. Lawrence Pound, and if the loony wanted to leave the fortified area and go where hundreds of thousands of people consumed by fear were on the edge of insanity, well, what the hell, let the bastard through.

Pound drove wildly through the last gate that was guarded with tanks and quad-mounted machine guns. The officer in charge shut down the electrical charges to the mines that covered the road and every square foot of ground to either side. The moment the racing car went past the last mine, the current surged back; any pressure would detonate the deadly mines.

A mile away, Pound began to see people camped by the roadside—grim, frightened animals who cringed with every blast of wind, every roar of thunder, every tremble of the earth beneath them. But Lawrence Pound gave them only a glance. He must reach the tent where El-Asid gathered his flock to him, where he preached the only true word, that Star Bright must be destroyed, that if the world were to survive, then the satanic minions— Kimberly, Clayton, Tretyakov, and the rest—must be killed at once. So long as they lived, God would scourge this world, and they would all be lost. This was the test, this was the Word, that man must not kindle on his own the elemental forces of God Himself.

Lawrence Pound knew the weaknesses in the defenses, he knew where to lead El-Asid and the others, he was aware of how they could penetrate even the deadly defenses. He must do this, he must.

His car slowed. People crowded everywhere, many of them with their clothes torn, their faces haggard. He felt compassion for them and knew the fear they suffered. But he would free them, one and all!

Men had cowered too long. It was past time for the dominant race on the planet to quit being so subservient to science and its satanic meddlers. It was past time for the human animal to end the shivering through its rump, to stop howling so fearfully at the moon. They needed understanding, and he could bring it to them.

He *must* speak with El-Asid, he must let him know about the tunnels that carried the cables, tunnels through which armed men, carrying weapons and explosives, could pass beneath the guards and the barbed wire, and emerge in the midst of the fusion project headquarters. The great Trojan

Horse was now in the form of tunnels and conduits, waiting only to be filled with men to wreak their punishment on those who were offending the Lord.

Armed men stopped him, dragging him from his car. Wild-eyed and angry, he screamed his name, showed his identification badge, and shouted at them to release him. "Take me to El-Asid!" he screeched. "I must talk to him! I have information he needs!"

Rough and angry, the men hauled him ungraciously up a slope and through a mob that parted like a waving curtain. Pound heard a voice riding the wind, slipping beneath the almost constant peals of thunder, a voice launched by loudspeakers, crackling and breaking up, but a voice with meaning to it, with wonder and authority, railing against the monsters inside the government reservation. He heard only some of the words, but they were beautiful, for El-Asid was telling the people they must all hurl themselves against the defenses of Star Bright, or they would all, every last man, woman, and child in the world, die.

Then the voice went silent. Dazzling lights blinded Pound. Wincing in pain, he put up his arm to protect himself. He saw a blurred form. Someone was taking his identification card to El-Asid. Thank the Lord. El-Asid would listen. Once he knew who Lawrence Pound was, once he understood that he held the secret, he would listen, and together they would rally these good people—

"We have him!" a voice shrieked. "We have the worst criminal of all! Lawrence Pound himself! The arch-conspirator, the man who runs the filthy project! Here he is!"

Pound was confused. "No, no! A mistake, you're making a mistake! I came here to help you, I came here to help! *Listen to me*—!"

"As it was done in biblical times, so it must be done now!" Through the glaring lights, Pound saw the robed, bearded figure pointing at him with outstretched hand.

"He is evil! He must be destroyed by stoning! Men and women, heed me! *Cast the stones!*"

Pound shrieked, but rough hands battered him to the ground. He raised a hand to beseech El-Asid, to make him understand.

The first rock caught him on the side of his mouth, tearing away the skin and breaking several teeth. The pain was intense. There was another blow at his temple. He knew he was screaming. He felt a warm wetness between his legs. Oh, God, had he soiled himself? He could never—

Something smashed into his eye, a flurry of blows struck him in the chest, he tasted the salt of blood, and then all was pain, thuds, kicks, and thin screaming curses from far away.

"He's dead. The son of a bitch didn't last long, did he?"

"Go! Destroy! Strike now!"

The men and women began to move like a swarm of ground-hugging locusts. They carried rifles, shotguns, pistols; wrecking bars, poles, and rocks; home-made Molotov cocktails; cans of oil and gasoline; dynamite—anything that could destroy and kill. A human sea flowed over the roads and the fields, a mass tide of two-legged lemmings, ready to accept their own destruction if necessary. Their throaty roar mingled with the flash of lightning and the blasting thunder, spurring them on, inflaming their anger and their fear, and they swept down upon the heavy fortifications. They did not fear what waited for them, for another fire burned in them, the flame of dedication; they were determined to destroy the heresy. They were frightened, and they had seen the wand moved by God, the bolts of lightning that bridged one world to another. They had their Sign. Their trucks preceded them—heavy trucks loaded with gravel and oil and having bulldozer blades attached to ward off bullets and to protect the drivers long enough to get to the barbed wire and the barricades. A dozen of them one after the other, engines screaming, rushed at eighty miles an hour straight at the gates.

The first radio-controlled mines went off, then more, and still more until gasoline-fed explosions tore skyward. But the mob did not stop. It surged ahead, stumbled and ran, fell and got up. Their roar beat back the thunder from the sky. Once off the paved roadway, however, they had to slow down, for the underbrush was thick and the ground hilly.

They struggled forward—directly into the line of fire of more than a hundred Vulcan cannons, each with a firing rate of six thousand rounds per minute. A Vulcan is like no other weapon in existence. It is an electrically operated Gatling gun that fires so fast the weapon has the sound of a giant rattler. Its effect is devastating beyond belief.

More than thirty-eight hundred people died in the first few seconds of firing. Another ten thousand, perhaps more, were instantly mutilated or wounded. The huge mob moved slower, but its own momentum was now its worst enemy. It could not halt its sluggish movement directly into the weapons, although thousands of people began streaming away to the sides. However, there was no darkness to hide those escaping, not with lightning flickering constantly and with the heavens themselves aglow.

Also, there were the eye-stabbing searchlights of a hundred turbine-powered killer helicopters playing on them. From the air, the human horde looked like a herd of small buffalo in slow motion. The helicopters came down in loose formations, engines howling, dazzling lights stabbing and pinioning their helpless prey, and they opened fire.

A hundred airborne Vulcan cannons went off and small rockets, with the punch of heavy artillery shells, were fired. They were terrifying, inescapable, weaving and bobbing in the air, snarling with high-pitched jet screams, howling with rocket fire and the BRRRRRTTTTT! of the rotating cannon. They fired for only forty-five seconds, and when the rockets were spent and the Vulcan barrels red-hot, more than twenty thousand bodies littered the countryside.

After the attack, General George Sebastian dry-heaved again and again until he felt his own entrails would disgorge through his burning throat. But there had been no other way. If they had let the mob escape with only mild punishment, they would only regroup, flog themselves back into a frenzy and return.

From news reports, Sebastian knew it was the same all over the world. The human race was going mad, and he couldn't blame them. Every nuclear power station in the world had been attacked and destroyed by screaming, enraged, terrified waves of what had been human beings. Engineers, secretaries, janitors, technicians—it didn't matter. They had been hacked, mutilated, dismembered and killed wherever they were found.

Goddammit, Sebastian thought, it didn't matter one way or the other, because they'd all damned well be dead within a week, anyway.

Leaving his command bunker, he went outside and looked up at a huge tongue of lightning flashing a quarter of a million miles from his world to the moon. Good God, he thought, you could watch it moving through space to the moon! The beauty of it struck him, a thought he hadn't expected. The beauty of it . . .

He looked out onto the hills where the killer choppers weaved slowly. In the distance, under their searchlights, he saw that the hills were mostly red.

It took a lot of blood to do that, a whole hell of a goddamned lot of blood.

Calmly, completely at peace with himself, General George Sebastian unhooked the .38 revolver at his hip, withdrew the weapon from its holster, cocked back the hammer, placed the muzzle in his mouth, and pulled the trigger.

17

Wind gusts slammed at the thick windows of the research center, sending a gloomy moan rattling through the frames. Owen Kimberly looked up and offered a wan smile to Angela as she brought steaming coffee to him. Over her shoulder, he saw the ever-present lightning crackling through the air. Angela placed cups before the others, and Tretyakov, Clayton, and Kathy Farrel sipped gratefully. They were numb from long hours spent with their computers, which were hooked up via ground cable to the giant computer system of the National Security Agency outside Washington.

For the first time since the nightmare had begun, they had hard answers to the questions that had so bedeviled them. For the first time, but perhaps not in time. Now they waited for a closed-circuit television link directly with President Arthur Whiteson in the White House. Their conversation had to be directly with the president, for no less than his authority could cull from the madhouse that had become the nation what amounted to the one desperate chance they had determined from the computer studies.

Eighty-four hours.

The number drilled through their heads, clinging like a dark mental leech within their minds. The last eighty-four hours for them and all the world, perhaps. If they failed to extinguish the tiny black star before that time, they would never know the eighty-fifth hour.

Already the great whirlwinds were sweeping the countryside. The electromagnetic and ionization effects had been bad enough. Now the heat was seeping through the magnetic sheath surrounding the microstar and was swept up along with the towering blue funnel into the atmosphere. The convection effects were staggering, giving birth to monster thunderstorms that towered to ninety thousand feet above the land, joining in huge and violent weather fronts. Violent winds tore the land, and black, menacing squall lines, bulging with malignant energy, rumbled like tidal waves through the air. Then came the worst of all—the brigades of tornadoes. They came in bunches, spiraling killers looking like braided ropes or impossibly long vacuum cleaner hoses, twisting and writhing as they swept the countryside, destroying land, buildings, and people. At other times, huge spinning masses, some of them several miles in diameter, gouged the earth before their path as if they were monstrous drill bits spinning at thousands of revolutions per minute.

The world had become a bedlam of lightning-spat thunder, raging storms, and the locomotivelike roars of tornadoes, all played to the deep thrumming sound of the electrical funnel that hurled its lightning through the air and screamed to the moon.

Yet all this would be only mild prelude if the black star were permitted its growth. Its density had already wrinkled and scarred the earth, and its descent into the crust, measured at first by no more than theoretical calculations, now could be detected in terms of inches. If it continued in this fashion, the magma beneath the crust would be affected and would start to boil violently, which would increase the speed of descent of the black star and the collapse of the earth's crust.

With the insatiable pattern of increasing mass and increasing release of energy, the microstar would fall toward the center of the earth. Micro would explode to macro and in that single, utterly savage instant, the earth would become a new sun.

But now, at last, there was hope, a single chance that had emerged from the long tapes of intensive computer calculations and from the interplay of ideas among Kimberly, Clayton, Tretyakov, and Farrel. It *might* work. Might. But it was the single, last hope.

A technician buzzed the scientists. "We have a connection with the president. Will you please put on your sets?"

They placed headsets over their ears. Small boom mikes were moved before their lips, and television cameras were readied. The scientists and several technicians, all wearing the same gear, studied the television screen before them.

The president appeared on the screen. Owen Kimberly was shocked. Whiteson's face was gaunt, strained, his eyes heavy, a nervous tic showing in a muscle along his left cheek.

For the moment they stared at their respective television screens. Kimberly spent a moment accepting that he might look even worse to the president than the frayed man did to him. He shook himself free of his thinking. They simply didn't have any time to waste.

"Owen, gentlemen, ladies," Whiteson said quietly. His voice was hoarse, yet it carried strength, and that buoyed Kimberly's spirits. "I understand we may have a last gasp."

At least no one was wasting time. Kimberly almost laughed aloud at the absurdity of the remark in his head. But there was no levity in his voice.

"Yes, sir," he replied. "It's a thin chance at best, Mr. President. And whatever we do it must be less than eighty-four—no, make that less than eighty-three hours—from right now. By the end of that time, we won't be able to—to—" His voice faltered, and Whiteson stepped in.

"What do you need, Owen?"

"We need artillery, sir. A certain type of artillery."

The president didn't respond immediately. It was obvious he couldn't believe what he had heard. Even in their mad world, the bizarre still numbed. "Artillery?" he echoed. "I want to be absolutely certain of what you're saying. There won't be time, obviously, for us not to be right from the beginning."

"Yes, sir," Richard Clayton broke in, his voice high, nervous and wavering. "Kimberly's right. We need to create a mass sufficient to break up the fusion fire. Despite how fast it has grown, it's still in a delicate balance. We've got to fracture that balance, Mr. President! We've got to . . ." His voice rose even higher, then faded away. Clayton stared with wide, hollow eyes, a nearly transparent salamander, at the screen.

Arthur Whiteson, noting Clayton's state, directed his next question to the Russian scientist. "Mr. Tretyakov, are you in agreement with this need for artillery?"

The Russian nodded vigorously. "I am agreeing with Kimberly," he said without hesitation. "If you will permit, Mr. President, I am the general in high command for artillery in Russia." Tretyakov paid no attention to the sharp looks he knew he must be receiving from the others in the control room with him; he had known the news would be no surprise to the American president, who would have known virtually everything about him before he had arrived in the United States. Tretyakov went on.

"We have made calculations," he said in his rumbling voice. "If we can fire, from many directions and at the same moment, a heavy mass into the tiny star, then it is possible, you understand? We can promise nothing, but there is a good chance this mass, created in an instant, can also disrupt the time-space factor. It may close off what we call the pinhole between two times, two universes and—" The Russian shook his head violently.

"Forgive me, if you please," Tretyakov broke in on his own words. "I do not mean to lecture, only to justify for you what we think, we calculate, why we need—"

Suddenly the room was jolted. Everything blurred before them for a moment, and dust drifted through the air. When it cleared, they still saw the president's face on the screen, but heard no sound. Moments later a technician handed a telephone to Kimberly and another to Tretyakov. On the screen they saw the president picking up a telephone. At least they still had direct connection for conversation and could still see one another.

"I think it's best if we get right to what we need," Kimnberly said at once. "We don't know how long this connection will last—we're getting serious ground displacement here. We're ready to give you requirements. It will take your authority, Mr. President, to get these things to us immediately."

"Go ahead."

Kimberly motioned to Tretyakov, and the Russian picked up the phone. "I know your weapons," he said. "We need your anti-tank weapons—Your new Mark IV tank killers, Mr. President, with their 106-mm high-velocity, flat-trajectory guns. They must have solid projectiles. The shells we need in particular are Mark Nine."

They saw Whiteson nodding slowly. "You are well informed, Mr. Tretyakov."

"At the moment I am very glad it is so," Tretyakov said blandly.

"I agree. How many?"

"Forty-five. We need them at once so that then we can move them into place, secure them properly, use lasers for alignment. We can use the computer for the final count so firing will be simultaneous. I ask for forty-five. Thirty-seven might do the job, so we are leaving extra for good measure."

"Are you agreed, Owen?"

"Yes, sir. Especially about the immediacy and the need for your intervention. You see, we still have measurements to make. Our plan is to shut down the magnetic sheath at the same instant the guns fire. By bringing those projectiles at super velocity into the same space at the same time, we'll be creating a rather powerful implosion mass of our own, and we may be able to disrupt the warp we—"

"Never mind that now, Owen, I don't need to know any more. Can you connect me with General Sebastian right away?"

Kimberly and Tretyakov glanced at once another. The Russian shrugged. Kimberly looked up at the screen.

"General Sebastian killed himself, sir."

Whiteson nodded slowly. "I understand. I heard the reports, and—all right. I'll get Sam Holzer at Fort Bragg. He's got the airborne forces under him, and he'll have everything you need. Gentlemen, I'll attend to it at once. In the meantime, have your people open several lines from your center to my office and keep them open every moment for any further communication. Is there anything else?"

"No, sir," Kimberly said.

"Good luck." The screen went blank.

Kimberly rose to his feet. "Let's get to work." Suddenly he fell to his knees, struggling for balance as another shock wave rattled the room. It felt as if the microstar were mocking their last-gasp effort.

18

Major General Sam Holzer climbed onto the small stage for crew briefings. His boots glistened in the overhead lights, every uniform crease drawing a sharp line. He wore not a single ribbon, although his men knew that in full-dress uniform those ribbons added up to at least seven rows. What he did wear spoke for itself—combat infantryman's badge, paratrooper wings, pilot wings. Sam Holzer was a soldier first and a general second, and at this moment that attitude could be very important to the pilots, air crews, tank crewmen, and paratroopers assembled before him. He wore a small microphone clipped to his starched collar.

Sam Holzer seemed to be paying little attention to his men, but both he and they knew otherwise. These men were spooked. No doubt about it, he thought. The whole country was spooked, and half the world had gone ape. He was going to brief these men, and he damned well wasn't going to make a speech. If they failed in what they had to do, a fair number of these troops were going to be dead soon. Christ, stop getting ahead of yourself, he snapped in sudden self-recrimination.

"Gentlemen." The one word was sufficient to bring instant silence to the hundreds of men before him.

"Gentlemen, as you know, while you are attending this briefing, your loading crews are moving Mark IV vehicles aboard the C-130 aircraft at Bragg. Your assignment is to fly those weapons, with full ordnance, to the two airfields of the Cumberland Reservation of the Atomic Energy Commission." He waited for the stir to rise and then to subside. They all knew about Cumberland.

"We all know what the weather is like closer to that funnel. It stinks. It's worse than that. It is plain damned horrendous. I want you pilots to understand there will be no altitude flying. You leave here, and you fly on the deck, and you stay on the deck. No cloud or weather penetration. The winds are crazy the closer you get, and the place is full of funnel clouds, lightning, and the rest of it. Anybody who gets caught in that stuff hasn't much of a chance of getting down. In addition, your avionics won't be worth tits on a boar. Nothing is working. The ADF, VOR, ILS—all systems are hash. It's eyeball all the way, and you'll fly your patterns into the fields exactly as if you're in a combat situation. I don't care if you tear up your airplanes just so long as those Mark IV vehicles make it safely to the ground inside Cumberland. Each aircraft will have a full complement of paratroopers. They will be armed, and they *will* have live rounds in their chambers. Once you're on the ground, if anybody interferes with moving those vehicles to their delivery points—you'll be met on the ground for that—you will cut them down *and ask no questions.*"

Sam Holzer held his words for a moment. He couldn't get away from the rest of it. Well, dammit, there wasn't any reason to.

"Gentlemen, I believe you should share with me the knowledge that this mission was assigned to me personally by the president of the United States. Personally," he emphasized, "by our commander in chief. I was informed that the Mark IV vehicles will not be used for any combat activity of any kind. They are not intended to shoot at people, but they *must* be delivered to Cumberland. Apparently they are needed in whatever attempt is being made to destroy the energy force—or whatever the hell it is that's going on down there— that is already starting to wreck the world. You troops know I don't go for gung-ho speeches and all that claptrap. But I won't be exaggerating one bit if I tell you, from what I was told today by the president, that if we don't carry out our assignment successfully, next week may never happen."

The men had heard rumors, but hearing those words from Sam Holzer was as big a shock as being hit by a lightning bolt. So what they had heard was true.

"Any questions, gentlemen?" Holzer looked up and down and across these men of whom he was so proud. No one made a sound.

"Very well, then. You have your mission to fly. I will be in the lead aircraft."

Before he could leave the podium, one man shouted suddenly, "Hell, general, we know *that!*"

*   *   *

Sam Holzer ordered the men to move 110 Mark IV tank killers with their 106-mm high-velocity weapons to Cumberland. Even though he knew that only forty-five vehicles were needed, Holzer figured they would take more than fifty percent losses in the hellish weather surrounding the two Cumberland airstrips. He assigned half the powerful Hercules turboprop transports to one field and the second half to the other. The men had also marked off two golf courses and a large open area as emergency landing sites.

With its powerful engines and prop reversers, a Hercules could be dumped almost anywhere. Then it was just a matter of lowering the ramp in the aft belly of the ship and driving out the Mark IV's. Mission accomplished.

There had been a last-minute addition to their cargo. Each transport would carry a dozen fully pressurized suits with internal liquid-cooling systems. These had been rushed to Bragg by jet transport from the space center in Houston.

A small crowd moved to each Hercules, but three men formed the nucleus for each aircraft. They busied themselves with the immediate problems both of their flight and their mission; determining how much fuel was to be carried, the center of gravity of the transport with its heavy load, and their cruising speed (altitude: minimum); selecting the charts they would need; checking details of the landing strips; and performing various other necessary tasks. They would try to communicate with one another by UHF in the hopes that the ultra high frequency radios would get through the violent electrical storms. Knowing the maelstrom that awaited them, each crew gave meticulous attention to the hold-down clamps and cables for the heavy tank killers and ammunition stores.

At last the great camouflaged aircraft were ready to go. Wind gusts tried but failed to drown out the screeching cry of auxiliary generators feeding power to the aircraft.

As modern aircraft went, the Hercules was about as aesthetic as a rock. Its wing rested across a cavernous fuselage, its four powerful jet engines turned fat-blade propellers, and the machine rested on a bulky housing of landing gear in thick pods. Yet the men climbing into their airplanes were confident in every inch of the stout metal frames, for the Hercules was a brute, and anything less than this machine would have little hope of surviving what lay ahead. Along the flight line, men clambered up steps, ascended steep, short ladders, and moved into another world, the flight decks of their aircraft.

Engines turned, propellers spun faster and faster and bit into the air with a deep, thrumming cry, and the aircraft moved away from their parking spaces, spraying and splashing water from side to side as they rocked in slow-motion. Then they were turning onto the active runway, every plane lit brightly with wing-tip lights, rotating red beacons, landing lights, and flashing strobes. They would have to remain visible in the air, for they were all flying due west across the Smokies to the Cumberland Gap. In normal weather, a flight could cross those mountains with feathery ease. Normal was yesterday. Today was stormy skies, death at higher altitudes, and the need to punch through on the deck.

One after the other, the planes rose into the turbulent air, wings trembling, crews strapped in tightly, knowing it was going to be an absolute bitch.

It was. Some of the Hercules crews tried to work their way through passes in the hills and mountains, but it was a near-suicidal attempt because the clouds came down wetly to hug the killer peaks. Other transports ran into rain so violent they couldn't see their own wing tips. Flying blind, the pilots on the gauges, and they had no choice but to go *up*.

There, jagged tongues of electrical force whipped freely from their battlements. Lightning flashed and exploded wildly in the gloom that swept down upon the winged machines, turning the powerful aircraft into miniscule toys fighting for survival.

The men in the planes had entered a world that all their experience had never prepared them for—they had become children subjected to the flickering appearance of lethal goblins casting a constantly flickering gleam all about them. The transports picked up tremendous electrical charges, and they began to glow with the static electricity suffusing every inch of the violently tossed wings. Electrical fire spattered from propeller tips, danced along the wings, gathered in fiery clouds on the radomes, and flickered in ghostly blue and red in the cockpits and the great cargo holds.

One hundred and ten machines flew into the great squall lines, storms that had burst all their bonds and rose to a hundred thousand feet above the earth. The storms swallowed the great airplanes, smashed at them with rain and hail, and hurled them about with turbulence so wild that steel cables snapped and the heavy Mark IV tank killers hurtled free and ripped through fuselage sides, tearing their carriers apart. Of the first forty planes to penetrate the storm front, nineteen never made it across the Great Smokies.

They had rushed into a raging sea of lightning, an ocean of liquid, screaming fire. Sam Holzer died in the lead Hercules when a searing bolt of lightning speared the machine and ripped open a wing. The plane burst into flames and fell to the earth below.

Turbulence hurled the transports about, and men in the planes were tossed about so violently that they broke arms and legs. The storms switched from positive to negative forces so abruptly the men's bodies could no longer contain the savage change in weight of their body liquids; noses and ears spurted blood, and men cried out in pain. Some pilots were unable to fly their machines, and planes were dashed like fragile toys against slopes or simply torn apart in the air.

Worst of all were the tornados, the killer funnels unseen by the alarmed pilots charging from one raging storm to another until it was too late. A twister would snatch at the airplane and with contemptuous ease, like a man plucking the wings of a fly, would snap away the great metal shapes, leaving the transport to spin madly out of control until it exploded against the earth.

Yet, with airplanes coming apart beneath their hands, some pilots fought through the gauntlet of storm fury, lightning, killer tornados, and upreaching hills. They lurched from the terrible skies and slammed onto the airstrips in Cumberland, carrying the machines that were the last hope for saving the human race.

"All right, Vasily. Turn around. Can you hear me?"

Vasily Tretyakov turned slowly, his thick body encased in a pressure suit with its own oxygen backpack, heavy armor, and liquid-cooling systems. Through the radio in his helmet, he heard Kimberly, and he nodded as he replied.

"Very good, Owen. You come in clear."

"The suit checks out. I think you'd better give me a final eyeball check." Kimberly turned slowly as the Russian studied the other suit then nodded in satisfaction.

"We look like we're walking on the moon," Tretyakov noted. And indeed they did. The suits were heavy and cumbersome, but well protected against the rising heat, the winds, and, to some extent, against radiation.

"The moon?" Kimberly shook his head, a slow motion seen through the front visor, "More like Venus to me. A special brand of hell, I guess."

Tretyakov gestured with his right arm. "We go, all right? Other teams are already working."

They started walking together from the control building, moving at a slow but steady pace until they were exposed to the open. It took several minutes to accustom themselves to movement within the heavy suits, a task made all the more difficult by the fierce winds racing along the surface. They began their walk toward the line of armored vehicles that had been flown in.

"How many tank busters got through?"

Kimberly could barely see Tretyakov from the

rounded edge of his helmet. At the moment he started to answer, he tripped and stumbled clumsily. He would have fallen except for the powerful grip of his companion. "Thanks, Vasily. I've got to remember to watch every step." He started out again, carefully looking down at the ground.

"Less than fifty," he said finally, in answer to the other man's query. "Most of the planes went down trying to cross the mountains, and—"

Tretyakov wasn't interested in losses; only survivors. "How many got through?" he repeated.

"I understand at least forty-five. I can't be sure, It's a confused situation, and we *think* that's the number. We'll know in a few minutes, anyway."

Buffeted by the winds, they continued their slow progress, finally reaching a small slope that gave them a better direct study of the area before them. Some of the Mark IV tank killers were already in position, and others were clanking their way to sites marked by steel poles. Every man within the tanks, and these had fairly good protection, wore the same protective suit as Kimberly and Tretyakov, as did the men handling the bulldozers, which even at this moment were smashing down building walls and clearing paths for the Mark IV vehicles and their 106-mm high-velocity weapons.

The bulldozers had to work around the forcefield generators and the machines, and their task was made even more difficult because of the heavy dust that hurled up before being snatched away by the wind. They were actually within the perimeter of the funnel that howled skyward, and fortunately the worst of its energy moved above their heads. Yet it was a numbing sight to be so close to the churning, writhing thing, to feel the teeth-grinding sounds and energy fields. They had no choice but to concentrate on what they were doing.

So the bulldozers continued to demolish all obstructions in the circle where the Mark IV vehicles were to be positioned. Laser survey instruments had been used to mark off a perfect circle about the building where Star Bright was growing steadily in its strength.

Technicians were on the scene to position the gun-carrying tanks. Forty-three Hercules transports out of the 110 that had left Fort Bragg had made it into the Cumberland airstrips, but two crashed on landing. Now, forty-one Mark IV's moved under their own power into position where they would be locked in place, then secured with steel bolts and metal straps. Technicians aimed the powerful guns with laser survey instruments, all forty-one weapons locked onto a single point, a theoretical line-of-sight firing that came together precisely where the tiny star howled.

Kimberly and Tretyakov finally commandeered an armored personnel carrier. They were exhausted from trying to walk through the area to study several of the Mark IV tank killers, to determine if they were in the correct positions.

They rode slowly, their hair standing straight the closer they went to the energy source. Everything about them flickered and glowed. Their radios were useless, any signal turned into hash. They were able to talk by bringing their helmets into physical contact and letting vibrations carry sounds and words between them.

"Must go back!" Tretyakov shouted to Kimberly.

"Look at your radiation meter! We cannot stand more!"

"We've got to!" Kimberly shouted in return, knowing his voice sounded dull and muted, just as he heard Tretyakov's. "Dammit, Vasily, all these men are taking the same risk as us! They—"

"Don't be fool! If you or I are hurt now, all this could be waste!" Tretyakov grasped Kimberly's arm and shook it angrily. "Now is not the time to be a hero! We go back!"

Kimberly hesitated. He looked through the thick glass of the personnel carrier and felt his teeth grinding in helplessness. Out there men were trying lethal doses of radiation as they worked the bull-dozers, sacrificing their lives so others might live. They worked their powerful bulldozers with amazing skill. They were chewing down walls, brushing aside the crumbling debris. They had to knock down the walls to the main fusion laboratory and at the same time not cause any damage to the equipment inside. A hell of a job.

And they were doing it. As they watched, Tretyakov angrily tugging at Kimberly's arm, the last wall between them and the magnetic bottle tumbled down in a shower of bricks. Dust spun into the air, whisked away before the wind.

But without those walls to block the direct effects of the outpouring radiation, they were embraced by still another signature of the fusion fire. An unholy radiance streamed out, pulsing in tremendous color bands, nearly blinding them. Kimberly stared at new teams coming into the area within armored personnel carriers. They would be laying the heavily shielded cable from the control center and setting up the timing sequence system so that the weapons could be fired by the main computer. Then they would fall back and be ready at a moment's notice to go into the deadly area again if any of the weapon systems showed a fault.

Tretyakov pounded loudly on the back window of their carrier and motioned with violent hand signals for the driver to leave the area at once. They drove away with increasing speed, Tretyakov watching Kimberly slumped in his seat.

Behind the thick, protecting walls at their control room, he helped Kimberly from the carrier, then half-dragged him inside, where suit technicians released them from their bulky garments.

Tretyakov motioned to Angela. "Feed him at once. Hot soup, whatever you think is good to get back his energy."

"Did something happen out there? To Owen?"

Tretyakov shook his head. "He is disturbed, watching men working until they are walking dead from radiation. We need him able to *think*, Angie. There is no time to be nice or to be kind, you understand? Take him to the office, get him food. I will bring the doctor there, maybe for shots or medicine. Woman, do not waste time. Go."

She led Kimberly away. An hour later he was fast asleep on the couch in his office. When Tretyakov entered the office, Angela came to his side quickly.

"He's eaten, but he's absolutely exhausted. Do you understand, Vasily? Unless he rests, just a little, he'll be worthless. Let him sleep a couple of hours, and he'll—"

"One hour. No more."

"Vasily, you've got to understand! He's wiped out, he—"

"Then get the doctor to give him shots. It is you who do not understand, Angela. I have just come from Kathy Farrel and the computers. The ones we have here are no good. The electromagnetic field, it destroys programming. The memory systems are like borscht."

She understood. "Then all this is—is useless, isn't it?" she said slowly.

He shook his head. "No. There is still a chance. We need one more computer check. We *must* have it. Kathy explains there is a big industrial center maybe a hundred miles from here. We must go there, we must have this last test. I've talked with other people. The army has a very powerful jet helicopter. It will be here in one hour, and we must all be ready to go." He glanced at his watch. "Only one hour, Angela. Be ready."

19

"No! That would be complete insanity! Have you both lost your minds?" Richard Clayton, his hands moving nervously through the air, glared angrily at Vasily Tretyakov and Owen Kimberly.

"Don't you understand? If you both go and something happens to that helicopter, you've almost destroyed our chances." They saw Clayton literally grinding his teeth together. "Tretyakov, you stay here with us. Owen's worked longer than you have with Kathy on the programming. They'll go together and if something—happens to them, if they don't make it back, at least we'll have our own last crack at that thing out there."

"You are wrong," Tretyakov told him. "It is necessary we both go. We must—"

Kimberly moved closer to them, shaking his head, motioning for Dick Clayton to calm himself. "He's right, Vasily. We're both too strung out to realize what he's saying is true. If we can't get back from the Stanford center, then you and Dick can at least make the attempt. You can stretch out the last hours until you *know* there's no more waiting. But if we're both—" He turned suddenly to the four paratroopers who shadowed their every move now.

"Is everything ready?" he asked.

"Yes, sir. We've just checked. The crew is ready to move out the moment you and your people are on board."

Kimberly turned to Kathy Farrel. "You've got everything?"

She nodded and touched her attaché case. "It's all here."

"Let's go, then. Angie, you set?"

Angela Dobson stood quietly by his side. "I'm ready. But I hoped the—" She broke off as a man entered the control room. "Dr. Jackson! I'm glad you're—"

"What's he here for?" Kimberly demanded.

"He's going with us. Just in case," Angela said quickly.

Kimberly's eyes narrowed. A tremor shook the room and dust drifted about them. They hardly noticed the tremors anymore unless the jolt was enough to knock them from their feet.

Tretyakov took his arm. "Is it really necessary, this trip? Even a helicopter may not be enough. You know what the storm is like out there, Owen. Maybe—"

"We're wasting time we don't have," Kimberly snapped. "You stay here with Clayton. Goddammit, Vasily, that's an *order!*"

Tretyakov started to respond, his own anger flaring. Then he nodded slowly. A sad smile came to his face. "Take care, Owen."

They shook hands for a moment. Kimberly started to talk but changed his mind. He turned suddenly and started from the control room, the others hurrying after him.

They climbed into the helicopter that had landed outside on an open field. The powerful combat machine was jet powered, built for the most rugged duty. It was made to withstand severe punishment, but even here on the ground, the rotors turning, it trembled and swayed visibly in the slashing winds. The loadmaster checked their straps, tugging at the seat belts and shoulder harnesses. Above the roar of the engines and the wind, he assured them that the further they flew from their present position, the better their chances were.

They had 105 miles to fly to reach the industrial research center and the computers that had been cleared for their immediate use. The flight would take nearly two hours because of the fierce weather and the turbulent winds. Two hours for the flight, two hours with the computers, and two hours to get back. Six hours in all, and they had eleven hours ahead of them as a safety margin before they would run out of time.

The helicopter rose into the howling gale. Despite the seat and shoulder straps, they were badly shaken as the pilots struggled to keep the machine under control. They flew barely a hundred feet above the ground, rising and falling as was necessary. No more than several hundred feet over them, dark clouds raced by, a thick scud that, if they had flown above it, would have obliterated the ground below. The lower their altitude, the better was their chance for seeing and avoiding the screaming tornado funnels that could drop without warning from the clouds.

For the first forty miles, the flight was maniacal. More than once they thought their last moments of life had fled as the helicopter was buffeted and hammered. Through the windows, they saw the constantly flaring bolts of lightning, as well as the writhing funnels clawing their way across the heavily wooded countryside.

Then they were through the worst of it, and the turbulence eased perceptibly. White-faced, shaken to the core, Angela glanced at an equally frightened Kathy Farrel, who managed a brief but weak smile. In the thundering din of the helicopter, they had to shout to be heard, and neither woman was possessed of the strength to do so, save for an emergency. Kathy pointed at Owen.

Angela turned her head. By her side Owen was fast asleep, oblivious to the blows still raining on the helicopter, not hearing its jet scream.

"Thank God," whispered his wife. It was critical for this man to get any rest he could.

Security teams awaited them at the Stanford research center. "Dr. Kimberly, I'm Jack Marshall," a beefy man said in greeting. "Please come with me, sir."

They piled into a van, preceded by one armed vehicle and followed by another. "My apologies for the hardware, doctor," Marshall said, regarding the armed vehicles.

"Never mind," Kimberly told him. "Forget everything except the computers and our communications needs. Please. I don't want to sound officious, Marshall, but every moment counts."

"Yes, sir. We've had our orders directly from the White House." He assumed a professional air. "The computers are ready for you and Dr. Farrel. Our entire staff is here and at your disposal. The working tapes are cleared, and—"

"Good. How about the direct link with Cumberland?"

"We've got land lines open, but we can't vouch for how good they are or how long they'll stay open," Marshall responded, his brisk responses giving hope to Kimberly that they wouldn't waste any time here. "The problem is in surface shifting. Mild tremors, that sort of thing. But they're enough to break the cables."

"No microwave?" Kimberly doubted it but he'd cling to every last hope.

"No, sir, I'm afraid not," Marshall said to confirm his fears. "Same problem. The quakes have tilted the towers, and they're out of position, and with things the way they are—" He stopped, not finding it necessary to say what was obvious.

"Nothing else working?" Kimberly prodded.

"No, sir. Only the one land line and that, as I said, is pretty damned precarious. We've even tried direct communications satellite hookup. You know, the ATS system *and* the military comsats and God knows what else. Nothing."

"Well, we'll just have to hang on with that old-fashioned land line, then," Kimberly said, accepting the inevitable.

He hesitated, then turned back to the subject. "You understand why we've got to spend only minimum time here, Marshall. If those lines go out at any time, then our only hope is to get back to Cumberland with the information we obtain here."

Marshall nodded. "I don't envy you the trip, sir."

Kimberly looked at him sharply. "You might as well enjoy the envy, man. If we don't get back with the data we need, you may just not wake up tomorrow."

Marshall was taken aback by the remark. "I didn't know that—it had gone *that* far."

Kimberly gripped Marshall's arm. "I'm sorry. I didn't mean to say that just for effect. I did you an unkindness, Mr. Marshall. I should have kept my peace and—and—" He couldn't finish the sentence.

Marshall smiled thinly, taking a deep breath. "No. I'm glad you said all that. I'd hate to think I was being led like a lamb to slaughter."

Kimberly turned away to look through the van windows. He was startled to see large groups of people around, staring at the passing vans. "I'm surprised," he said slowly. "I thought places like this would be deserted. People do seem to have gone quite mad everywhere else, though God knows I don't blame them."

"We've always been tightly knit here," Marshall said proudly. "We're a very good research team here at Stanford, doctor. Oh, some people have left to be with their families. Those that could travel, that is. But the others, most of us—well, we've known things were bad, but not quite the way you put it. Anyway, there's been a consensus here that if everything comes unglued at the seams, we'd rather be here, surrounded by our own work, than running like the others." He smiled, a sad expression on his face. "The support staff—janitorial, services, that kind. Poor souls. They've been frightened to death by all this end-of-the-world talk, and they took off. So we've held it together by ourselves."

"Be damned glad you did. I know we are." Kimberly pointed ahead. "Is that it?"

"Yes, sir. The main computer room is in there. Everything's ready and waiting." The van slowed. The security guards were already out of the other vehicles, running ahead, weapons at the ready. But no one moved to harass or threaten them. There were only curious stares.

Inside, they went immediately to work. Kathy Farrel functioned as the alter mind for Kimberly, processing his data requests into the language understood by the computer. There was no simple way to handle the problem. As Kimberly received an answer to a problem, he immediately built upon this additional knowledge to formulate new queries. What he was trying to do was complicated at its start and brain-squeezing at its conclusion.

They had to take every aspect known of the fusion fire and attempt to predict precisely what would happen, along every instant of time, when they were ready to fire the high-velocity shells into the black star. There was never any hope of crushing the flame; you couldn't fight naked gravitational force with a fly swatter even if it was armor plated. What they were attempting to accomplish, on a scale of perhaps a millionth of a second, was an implosion of mass from every side of the microstar in the hopes they could still disrupt or unbalance whatever stretching of matter and energy was occurring.

They spent three hours with the computers.

Angela stood close by Kimberly, and during the long minutes when he could do nothing, as Kathy interpreted his questions for the programming language and he sat fretfully, she would move behind him to knead the knotted muscles in his neck and shoulders. It was little relief, but she understood the man and the strains that twisted within him; he would welcome any relief.

On the last session with the computer, Kathy Farrel remained, alone, locked in communication with the electronic brains for nearly forty-five minutes. No one could interrupt her; the technicians working with her were like doctors and nurses in an operating room. When she finally emerged, Angela looked at her and thought she would suffer a heart attack.

Kathy returned with her face white, her body trembling, to hand Owen Kimberly the final readout papers. He studied them, his body growing taut.

"You're certain?" he asked Kathy.

She nodded, still fighting for her self-control.

"According to this," Kimberly said slowly, "if we had followed our original plan, we would have—" His voice trailed away.

"Yes. We would have failed," Kathy Farrel confirmed aloud.

Kimberly glanced back at Angela. "Thank God we came here. What we were going to do would have ruined whatever hopes we have left."

He was on his feet, looking at Jack Marshall. "I'll need that telephone line, please. At once."

Marshall appeared stricken. "I'm sorry," he said, and his voice was strained, almost a hoarse whisper. "About twenty minutes ago, doctor. We lost contact, and—"

"*I've got to talk with Cumberland!*"

Kimberly's voice was so sharp, his anger so explosive, Marshall was unable to reply for a moment. He started to speak, swallowed air, then found his voice. "Sir, I understand, but there's nothing I can do! Or anyone else. We lost the land line, I guess because of a tremor—we don't know. We've tried everything to patch lines in a roundabout way. We've been trying microwave and radio, and we've even tried the satellites again. But there's nothing, nothing at all, and—" He took a deep breath again. "I'm sorry, Professor. Really, but—"

"The helicopter," Kimberly broke in. "Is it ready?" He turned to the four paratroopers who remained at all times in his presence. They were on their feet, waiting.

"It's ready, sir," replied their sergeant.

"Then I suggest we get the hell on that thing and on our way," Kimberly snapped, "and I mean *now*."

He didn't wait for a reply but went at a half-run from the room, not looking back to see who might be following. Angela and Kathy moved with him at once, and a startled Dr. Paul Jackson, who had promised himself never to get into that helicopter again, had to run to catch up.

Stepping outside the computer center, they were shocked to see the storm that had moved in. Sheltered within the building, they had known nothing of the driving wind, the gusts hurling the rain almost horizontally. Had they not known the time of day, it would have been difficult to separate day from night, so heavy and foreboding were the clouds. Lightning flashed and gleamed almost constantly, dazzling white-blue near them, yellow and murky in the distance, the glare cut down by the clouds and rain.

The crew slid open the hatch, and they clambered inside the helicopter. It rocked badly in the winds. They needed no urging to secure their seat belts and shoulder harnesses and to tie down their attaché cases and other bags, which could become flying missiles in the violent air. Moments later the engines started, and the great blades began to turn above them. The women sat quietly, hard against the backrests, waiting with the stoicism they had come to practice so well. Doctor Paul Jackson was a nervous wreck who seemed more in need of a tranquilizer than anyone else. Owen Kimberly had reached a state where anger had become a great solid mass all through his system. Weeks and weeks of frustration and swaying from hope to dismay, bouncing across the spectrum of extreme emotion, had taken its toll. Now at this final moment, when they had in their possession the all-critical information necessary to make their first and their only attempt to crush the black star, they were not able to communicate with Clayton and Tretyakov in Cumberland. He could no longer retain the calmness he had displayed through most of the pressure. He had only one thing on his mind: get this son-of-a-bitch helicopter back to Cumberland or die in the attempt.

Kimberly looked up to see the pilot coming from the cockpit toward him. He noted the man's nameplate on his flight suit. Major Bill Peabody.

"Professor Kimberly?" Peabody grasped something to balance himself in the severe rocking motions. "I must tell you, sir, we've lost all radio contact. With anywhere." Peabody's distress was obvious. "But one thing I can tell you for certain, sir. The weather was stinking before, but now it's gone to hell in a handbasket. Our chances for maintaining control aren't—"

"*Fly.*" Kimberly's teeth were gritted together. "Fly this thing to Cumberland. This instant, major. This very goddamned moment. Do you understand? And don't waste another minute talking to me or to anyone else about the weather!"

The major straightened slowly. He looked as if he were seeing the disheveled scientist before him for the first time. He lifted his right hand in a casual salute. "Yes, sir."

Within thirty seconds, they heard the engines screaming. There was no hope for anything resembling a normal takeoff. Peabody waited until they had full power, then turned into the howling wind, and "jumped" the chopper into the air with a violent lurch. Almost at once, the winds hurled them nearly on their side. Kimberly couldn't believe his own reaction.

Calm. Total commitment within himself. No more worrying about the winds, the tornadoes, the lightning. To hell with it all. Let that man up front fly this damned thing, and that was all there was to it. The headache that had nibbled at Kimberly for weeks was gone. He had sloughed off the mental dirt and the grubbiness in this single moment of coming to grips with himself, of rejecting everything save what had to be done. He was stunned with this inner peace, and at the same moment he didn't care one way or the other. Get back to Cumberland. *Period.* They'd either make it or not.

A flash of lightning gave everything within the cabin a stark, strobelike effect, and Angela was shocked when she looked at Owen. He stared through his window, his teeth bared in what looked like a snarl of defiance at all that was happening.

Kimberly was perhaps the only person aboard that machine who no longer felt fear or outright terror. Dr. Jackson, as they lurched crazily from the near-fatal vertical bank only scant feet over the ground, threw up. They heard his gasping sounds as he heaved, unable to lean forward because of the shoulder harness, his vomit splashing on his clothes, spraying in the air. No one could help him, not even when he began to choke and dry heave. He had to attend to himself, and for a while, white-faced and trembling, he did not even bother to wipe off his face with the sleeves of his jacket.

There was no air, no sky, no atmosphere, only the churning violence that, impossibly, worsened with every mile they flew. It was a repetition of their other flight, only worse. The severity of the storms increased with every passing hour. The lightning was constant, a display that banished darkness in violent fits and starts of naked energy.

Far ahead of them, closer to the horizon, the world was glowing. They could not see the great blue funnel churning upward; it was lost in the clouds that had laid a blanket only a few hundred feet above the ground. But beneath the base of the clouds its radiation had increased, and the horizon, like an enormous sliver lying beneath a bowl of blackness, beckoned to them with pulsating, multicolored waves of light.

Suddenly the horizon disappeared in rain so

thick they could hardly see. Down they went, the pilots unable to see anything to aid them in retaining their sense of direction. Within the cabin, electricity began to flow from one metal part to another, little trickles and fingers of static electricity taking form and shape, dancing and whirling in the air. Saint Elmo's fire. The static electricity so saturated everything it could not be contained or bled off from their machine. They smelled the danger, the imminence of their own destruction. The forces that had been invisible and now came to life in the form of dancing flame moved their hair out straight, irritated them, caused them to have a flat, metallic taste in their mouths.

Angela gasped as tiny blue flames crackled from her hair, lifting away from her head and face. Only a grim self-control kept the scream from issuing forth, and only her concern for Owen gave her that control. Fighting to keep her fear from consuming her, she brushed madly at glowing apparitions that were real.

Hurled up and down and from side to side, they endured a pounding. A wild skid snapped Kathy Farrel's head sharply against a bulkhead, and blood sprayed from her. Strapped in tightly, frightened, she automatically brought up her hand and pressed her own skin against the wound to stem the pulsing blood.

The air about them was gray, bluish, yellow, and green, a snarling web of constantly shifting bands of electricity.

Still they forged ahead. There was nowhere else to go, no escape, no safer route. Every foot they flew was a struggle through a living wall of maddened air, of invisible hammer blows that spun

them about so that sometimes they were almost
vertical, the nose of the helicopter pointing almost
straight down, the machine vibrating wildly through
its structure, the rotor blades flexing far beyond
their design limits. Just as quickly, their position
would be reversed, and they would spin madly.
The two pilots, soaked in sweat, fought just to
keep the helicopter from coming apart.

Kimberly noticed with almost casual interest that
three of the four paratroopers with them were
throwing up, their faces pasty white. He marveled
again at his own calm, his consuming drive to
reach the research center. That calm was given its
own test as a violent blow jammed his head down
into his shoulder blades, and he tasted blood from
where he had driven his teeth through the skin of
his lips. Still, he had that detachment, a mild
wonder at the skill of the pilots and at the durabil-
ity of this machine that flexed, groaned, and twisted.

They went through long moments when they
were totally out of control, feeling the emptiness
in their stomachs as they went through sudden
weightlessness and were then hurled violently
against the straps or slammed into their seats.
Mist sprayed through the cabin as they seemed to
fly through roaring waterfalls. Had there been some
enormous terrier in the heavens shaking them se-
verely in its teeth, their punishment could have
been no worse.

Yet the miles passed beneath them, the distance
to the Cumberland center growing ever shorter. It
was a race, a contest between downdrafts trying to
smash them into trees or ground and their own
power and pilot skill in staying aloft. It was an
endurance contest between the howling devils in

the air and the strength of metal. Objects flew about the cabin like shrapnel, but the passengers hardly felt the blows when they were struck. The physical movement was now so severe, so constant, that they were becoming numbed in body and mind.

It was never ending—time lost its meaning, breathing meant gasping and struggling for air, and sight was a nightmare of blinking into dazzling lightning and seeing the stinging sensations of afterimages.

Just when Kimberly was sure they were wallowing at the brink of total loss of control, he saw the lines of fortifications below, the barbed wire, the tanks and guns lined up. That meant they had passed through the outer defenses to Cumberland, that they were less than a dozen miles away from the building they needed so desperately to reach.

He realized then that even though his mind had found some peace, his body had reacted to the punishment. He was soaked through, some of it from his own sweat, some from the water that now came through every crack and sliver in the helicopter. He knew when another mile had gone by, and he began to mumble both prayers and curses in an unintelligible speech to himself.

Then came the blow the machine could no longer withstand, and he knew they were falling. The black horizon and its crackling tongues of lightning tilted madly, and Owen felt a terrible blow against his body. Suddenly wreckage was twisting and bending all about him, and they were lurching and pounding along the ground. Then his ears rang, but there was no movement. He heard the hiss of steam as rain pounded onto the hot engines and metal. His left arm hurt, felt as though a knife were twisting through it, and he knew it was broken. Dazed and in shock, he heard someone yell to get the hell out of here, but he couldn't move. Then two paratroopers were standing over him, one of them bleeding from a bad facial cut. They removed his straps and dragged him up from his seat. He started to protest and tried to say that he wanted them to get his attaché case with the papers but they dragged him from the wreckage. As they did, he noticed that they had the case.

Leaving him, the two paratroopers ran to help the women and the doctor from the wreckage. Stumbling and running, the paratroopers and the remaining passengers emerged from the wreckage. A few moments later, the fuel tanks behind them exploded with a whooshing roar. But they were safe from the flames.

Heat washed over Kimberly, and the driving rain, stinging his face as it did, was a blessed relief. He sat dazed, trying to struggle upward through the shock numbing his body as well as his mind. Looking up, he saw Dr. Jackson preparing a needle.

"What—what the hell is that for?" Kimberly choked out through his pain.

"Morphine. I've got to set your arm, and the pain is going to be—well, you'll need this."

"No!"

Kimberly clutched the wrist of the nearest paratrooper. "Orders," he gasped. "Have him set the arm. Hold me down if you have to." He nearly gagged from the pain. He sucked in air. "But no morphine, understand? Whatever happens, no morphine. And get me to the control center as soon as you can."

Through a blur he saw the trooper step before the doctor, heard them arguing, their voices drifting through the thunder. In the distance, as though in a dream, he saw a funnel cloud twisting along the horizon, hurling debris in all directions. It didn't bother him at all. Someone put a handkerchief, wrapped about wood, into his mouth. They held him tightly, and the doctor went to work with an emergency splint. Kimberly swore he wouldn't cry out. He didn't, but he fainted almost at once.

When he regained consciousness, he found that he was lying on the ground, his head propped in Angela's lap. The others were standing over him, watching. Kimberly blinked rapidly and inwardly cursed his own weakness. "Help me up," he commanded.

He swayed as he was brought to his feet, but he felt his head clearing rapidly. Beyond Angela's face he saw strangers, men in uniform, and beyond them a half-track, a powerful armored vehicle with wheels under the front section and tank treads making up the rear.

Kimberly motioned. "How far are we from control?" he asked.

"Four miles, sir." The speaker was a sergeant. He didn't seem to mind the howling winds or the rain slashing at him. By now, lightning and thunder were merely a backdrop instead of an overwhelming interference.

"Do you know who I am, sergeant?"

"Yes, sir. The others told me."

"That vehicle. Is it yours?"

"Yes, sir."

"Then get me into the damned thing, sergeant, and get me to control just as fast as you can."

"Yes, sir. We'll give it our best. The roads are a mess, but that thing can get through almost anywhere."

Kimberly nodded. "Good." He turned to Dr. Jackson. "What about the helicopter crew?"

"Badly hurt."

"Stay with them and do what you can. Farrel, you and Angela get into that half-track with me. Let's go, now."

Kathy and Angela helped him into the cab. Not until the door had closed and Angela was by his side, did he realize how fierce the storm had been all this time. The soldiers wrapped Kathy Farrel in waterproof canvas and huddled with her in the open back of the half-track. The vehicle set out slowly, climbing a small rise, its tracks gripping deeply into the muddy ground.

With an iron will, Kimberly hung onto his consciousness, Angela supporting him, trying to protect his arm. Kimberly gritted his teeth, closing his eyes with the pain, determined to overcome it. He knew that when they arrived at control he would need all the clarity he could muster.

Around the vehicle the wind was shrieking. Rain tore at the half-track, spattering and drumming off the thick metal. To each side of them, houses had been crushed by gales, trees were stripped of leaves, and debris littered the road and the countryside. There was an intermittent but ceaseless clanging of debris bouncing off the half-track. A lesser vehicle would never have survived the pounding.

As they rounded a curve, Kimberly realized

they had no more than a mile to go before they reached the control center. In the distance, down the slope, he saw, barely visible in the pounding rain, the buildings of the research center.

"Jesus Holy Christ!" the driver swore with mingled anger and fear as he slammed the accelerator to the floor, throwing them back in their seats. A cry of pain escaped Kimberly, and he and Angela turned to the driver, then looked out the window.

A whirling funnel cloud, spitting bluish static electricity and thundering like a thousand locomotives charged toward them. The half-track skidded wildly, the driver wrestling with the wheel, trying to by-pass the huge funnel cloud. Speeding wildly, the vehicle barely escaped the funnel cloud, which continued down the road, obscuring the world with its terrible power.

The driver slowed down, regaining control of the half-track. The rest of the way was downhill.

Angela pointed. "There, driver. See it? The building with the red signs. That's—"

"Got it," came the terse answer, and moments later they pulled up by the entrance.

They helped Kimberly down. He didn't waste even the time to thank the men who had brought them here, because even that was a luxury they couldn't afford.

Angela supported Kimberly and followed Kathy Farrel. They went directly to the main control room. Kimberly's entrance was an incredible shock to the people he had left here. Tretyakov and Clayton stared at him in disbelief, noting his torn, soaking clothes, his bruised face, and his arm in a sling.

"Owen!" The Russian cried his name and rushed

to him. He wanted to ask what had happened, but he knew this was not the time for inane questions.

"All that matters is that you have come back," he told Kimberly. "Everything is in readiness. All the weapons are emplaced, the sighting is confirmed. When we heard nothing from you, Owen, we gave you up for lost. We were about to start the final countdown. I am glad you are back now so you can work with—"

"Don't fire! Whatever you do, wait." Kimberly groped for a chair and was eased into it by Angela and Tretyakov. He looked up at the Russian and at Dick Clayton who had joined them.

"The computer run—we were right. If we go ahead as we planned, we would—we would be unleashing hell itself. We have to make some changes. We—"

"There is no time, Owen!" Tretyakov shouted. "We have less than an hour left!"

Kimberly pushed aside the coffee someone held before him. "We need only twenty or thirty minutes, Vasily, and we've *got* to wait."

"We can't risk it."

"We must. Or there's no hope." Kimberly struggled to his feet and walked painfully to the control panel, where he studied the electronic readouts. Without turning his head, he asked the question he needed answered. "Are we on final sequence?"

Clayton was by his side. "Yes, but—"

Kimberly reached out and hit the master cutoff switch.

A shriek of rage reached him almost the same instant that Clayton struck blindly at him. What felt like a white-hot poker smashed into his arm, and Kimberly fell helpless against the panel.

20

Kimberly sat quietly, waiting for the drug he had been given to take its effect. They had managed to get some hot soup into him, and then a doctor had injected a carefully measured dose of amphetamine into his system.

"It will give him two hours," the doctor explained to the others. "During that time, he'll be alert and thinking clearly. After that, either he gets some rest or he'll fall apart right before your eyes."

Kimberly smiled up at the doctor. "Thank you," he said, his voice broken and forced. But he was feeling better. The drug worked swiftly, and he could feel the energy surging through his system. He wanted to laugh aloud at the doctor's warning. Two hours? If everything they had struggled for wasn't completed in less than half that time, no one would worry about a thing.

"How's Clayton?" he asked. A grimace appeared on his face. "And what happened to him?"

Tretyakov looked down at him. "Something inside him snapped. When you cut down the system, Owen, he could not think straight. To him, because he has been here day and night, all the time, it seemed like you trying to stop what we doing up to now."

"How is he now?" Kimberly asked.

"Better. He has control."

"Get him here right away."

Kimberly walked, swaying only slightly now, and Angela, carrying soup, followed him. He stood before the long control panel, ignoring the rumbling beneath his feet, the crashing storm just outside. Moments later the team was assembled about him.

"What we found in the computer run," he said to the others, "is that we don't dare to shut down the magnetic sheath. If we do that, then the energy release may be so intense that the projectiles *could* be partially vaporized as they come together. And if that happens—"

He let it hang, and Tretyakov picked it up at once. A frown creased the face of the Russian. As quickly as Kimberly had made his brief statement, Tretyakov understood. "Of course," he said slowly. "If that happens then we get a flaw in the estimate of the final mass at the moment all projectiles are fired. Only very little flaw, but it could be enough."

"Precisely," Kimberly answered. "The implosion velocity, the very instant of everything coming together, could be thrown off just enough to destroy the very effect we're trying to achieve. And we'd fail."

For several moments, they absorbed that in silence. Lightning flickered in through the heavy windows. No one paid it any attention.

Kathy Farrel gestured with documents in her hand. "The only chance we have," she added, "is to fire directly through the magnetic force field."

"*Through* the field?" Dick Clayton was shocked by the statement. "Do you know how much energy is involved there? It's strong enough to bend what's coming out of that damned thing inside the bottle!"

"There's a critical difference," Kimberly told him. "We're deflecting what's essentially a plasma, or even with the heavier particles, it's still a current we're working with. When we fire inward, we're dealing in mass that's great enough to punch through. Everything depends, as you know as well as I do, on achieving the implosion mass as all the projectiles arrive at the same place in the same instant in time." He studied the panel. "That way," he added, "we can get the necessary mass where we want it before the shells are disrupted by the temperature inside the bottle. We may get some vaporizing of the surface of those things, but not enough to affect the timing."

"But what if you're wrong!" Clayton cried. His eyes were hollow, pools of inner agony.

"Then, Dick, you won't have much longer to worry about it, will you?" He looked at the others. "Let's get started."

The digital clocks on the walls of the control room and on the panels had become the enemies, electronic hourglasses through which their final grains slipped with frightening ease. The scientists had set up a countdown timer that ticked away the

minutes and seconds remaining. Kimberly glanced
at it. Glowing numbers stared back at him.

46:13

Forty-six minutes and thirteen seconds, and even
as he watched, mesmerized by the flickering
changes in seconds, the seconds slipped to 00, and
the minutes began falling away.

But there was no way to rush. They must go
through an elaborate procedure, the intricate rit-
ual demanded by the computer and the complexities of the systems with which they worked. Twenty
minutes dragged by. The ground tremors were
now more frequent, until it seemed they were
enduring a constant shifting and trembling beneath them, the final stirring of the great beast
coming to full life.

And with every passing moment, as the black
star gained in mass and increased the lash of its
outpouring radiation, the storm raging about them
grew wilder. The electrical hum from the blue
funnel was a constant buzz in their ears, and the
electromagnetic radiations had crawled behind their
eyeballs and in their sinuses until it seemed they
were all infested with hordes of tiny, snarling wasps
that threatened their sanity. There was now a very
real danger that the tornadoes charging across the
landscape could strike the building in which they
worked or disrupt the Mark IV weapons or even
the magnetic bottle that pulsated fiercely with its
shifting hues. In many more ways than their countdown, time was slipping away from their grasp.

"Twenty-two minutes, Owen."

Kimberly looked up, startled, as he heard the
quiet words, spoken almost with a hush from
Tretyakov.

"I know," Kimberly said.

"We are in danger from the storm, Owen. Is there any way to speed up our process?"

"Not until we're on automatic sequencing."

Tretyakov nodded slowly. "I understand. It is just," he sighed, "that now I know what it is like in Dante's Inferno. You must run to escape whatever is chasing you, but your feet are in mud, and everything is slow motion."

Kimberly showed a crooked grin. "Well put, Vasily. If we make it through this, you ought to take up poetry."

"I *am* a poet. But you do not speak or read Russian." Tretyakov gestured at the control panel before which Kimberly sat. "You make music with this."

Lightning crashed off the top of the building, soaked up by conductors, splashing harmlessly down the sides of the structure. But it was enough to paint their faces in that strobe effect that had become so familiar, yet was still so unnerving. They knew the scene was one familiar to hundreds of millions of people throughout the world. For weeks the planet had been host to vast streamers of electrical energy running amuck. Huge auroras filled the heavens everywhere, and when these were obscured by the thick storms, the clouds themselves glowed and cast forth their barrage of lightning and thunder. Whirlpools of naked energy swept earth and heaven. People's deepest fears and superstitions had emerged from their subconscious minds, almost, it seemed, in direct proportion to the fury raging across the planet.

Few men realized, however, that in this one building in Tennessee, itself beset by storm violence, the last minutes remaining were clicking away on digital counters.

"All right, everybody." They turned, hearts pounding, at Kimberly's words.

"It's now or never," he said, his voice carrying through the control room. "We're about to go on automatic sequencer to fire the guns. In ten seconds . . ."

The counters read 3:10, then flashed away the remaining seconds. When the counters read 3:00, a green light came on above the master control panel.

Three minutes to Truth.

The scientists' eyes swept over the gauges, the readout counters, everything that related to the thousands of calculations, checking off details, arranging hundreds of precision maneuvers, each of which must follow one after the other in perfect sequence.

The computer moved with maddening slowness. The people in the control room stared in a glaze of helpless, enervating horror, hearts pounding, nails digging into palms. Some people wept silently, unable to control themselves any longer. Every second was a lifetime.

Then the ground rocked sharply beneath them, and the scientists stared at a panel. *The gravitational pull from the black star was soaring.*

"We can't wait!" Kimberly shouted. He leaned forward over the master control.

The room shook. "It's the fire—" Kimberly's voice was a hoarse gasp—"It's descending. The mass is increasing faster than we calculated!"

He didn't need to say the rest. The star was beginning its descent into the earth's crust. Its mass was multiplying, squaring, increasing now with frightening speed. As it began its fall toward the center of the earth, it would destroy the structure of the crust. Whatever was nearby would fall toward the sinking black star, tumbling into the void left behind.

The next quake could be too much. The heavy weapons would be displaced and would no longer fire true.

Kimberly threw himself forward to the master control, his good arm extended. His hand slammed against a switch marked OVERRIDE. Then he spun to his right, his hand striking out again, hard against a red switch marked FIRE.

Aimed at the same point in space-time, every gun fired. A wicked lash of sound rippled at the building from outside. The shock wave cracked windows and hammered at their ears.

In a split second the heavy projectiles came together. Those in the control room stared at the television monitors. All they saw was a savage glare blanking out the screens.

The blinding light began to fade. The world rocked sharply. Then they felt something *different*— a pulse, a grinding through time. They heard an unnatural groan, and they knew they faced the impossible.

The walls of the building cracked wide. They saw only a blur as the earth heaved and trembled.

They heard, felt, *knew* the scream. It was a sound never before heard on the planet, the voice of strange and terrible gods crying out in torment and anger, a bellow of agony that shrieked from Elsewhen and pulsed once, overwhelmingly, to Now.

The cry of a billion dinosaurs sundered the heavens.

There came an enormous flash of light, beyond color, beyond knowing, beyond all understanding.

A spear whipped away from the earth, a single pulse of energy that flashed from here to "somewhere" so swiftly the pulse seemed like a spear reaching out to infinity.

The light went out. There was blackness.

The fire was out.

Time wrenched, blew itself apart.

The first scientists who lived far enough beyond what had been the research center to have survived the cataclysm arrived by helicopters many days later, when the earth was cool enough to allow their presence. They flew slowly, staring in awe and disbelief. What they saw—

They knew there must have been craters like this before, when the earth was still young, when it was still forming, and asteroids the size of mountains had rushed down from space to impact against the planet's crust.

It was a crater as large as any that had ever been formed, but yet it was different. It was nearly one hundred miles in diameter, the walls, slopes, sides and bottom were absolutely smooth, finer than the most perfect marble or glass ever made. It was glass harder than steel. Glass made within the crucible of a dying star.

The fire god had returned to the sun. *Star Bright* was gone.

Earth had been returned once again to man. There would be another chance to seed the future and bank the fires of civilization without bringing a star into the midst of man.

It was the first truly new start in almost two thousand years.